ON WILDERNESS
Voices from Maine

BORESTONE WINTER VIEW
Scott Perry

SCOTT PERRY has traveled throughout Maine for almost twenty years, working as a freelance photojournalist primarily for the *Associated Press* and *Maine Times.* With a continued passion for Maine's back roads and wild areas, he currently spends his time capturing landscapes on film in the panoramic format using specialized cameras. His work can be seen on the web at www. scottperryphoto.com.

ON WILDERNESS
Voices from Maine

EDITED BY PHYLLIS AUSTIN, DEAN BENNETT
AND ROBERT KIMBER

TILBURY HOUSE 🏠 PUBLISHERS
GARDINER, MAINE

Tilbury House, Publishers
2 Mechanic Street, Gardiner, ME 04345
800–582–1899 • www.tilburyhouse.com

First Edition: June 2003 • 10 9 8 7 6 5 4 3 2 1

Library of Congress Cataloging in Publication Data
On wilderness : voices from Maine / Edited by Phyllis Austin, Dean Bennett, and Robert Kimber.-- 1st ed.
    p. cm.
    ISBN 0-88448-257-X (pbk. : alk. paper)
    1 Natural History--Maine. I. Austin, Phyllis, 1941- II, Bennett, Dean B. III Kimber, Robert.
    QH105.M2 05 2003
    508.741--dc21

                                                                    2003006860

Cover designed on Crummett Mountain by Edith Allard, Somerville, ME.
Editorial and production by Jennifer Bunting and Barbara Diamond.
Color separations and scans by Integrated Composition Systems, Spokane, WA.
Printed and bound at Maple Vail, Kirkwood, NY.

Dedication

When co-founder John N. Cole first introduced the public to *Maine Times* on Oct. 4, 1968, he wrote, "Our journeys are one-way, one-time trips, and none of us is quite sure of his destination when the train leaves the station."

Surely John was headed for an unknown future when he left Long Island, New York, where he was a commercial fisherman, to move to Maine and become a newspaperman, editor and author. He could not know then that his destiny was to play a pivotal role in the new advocacy journalism of the '70s and to help define Maine's environmental agenda for decades to come. It was a fate that he enjoyed discovering every step of the way.

John was a gifted thinker on just about any subject, but especially about the environment. When he died on January 8, 2003, John left behind an impressive body of work—articles, essays, columns, books—that brought him national prominence and respect.

Maine's coastal bays and rivers were first in his heart, and John will be long remembered as a passionate advocate for clean waters and for restoration of the striped bass fishery. But he was also a tenacious voice for protecting the state's northern wildlands from overcutting and development, and he personally led a grassroots campaign to try to stop the state from opening a hunting season on moose.

We dedicate this book to John for his untiring efforts on behalf of the natural world and in appreciation for his unflinching courage to speak the truth as he saw it.

—Phyllis Austin

TABLE OF CONTENTS

iii   INTRODUCTION Phyllis Austin, Dean Bennett, Robert Kimber

1   ST. JOHN, WINTER Neil Welliver

2   WILDERNESS Neil Rolde

7   NOTHING BUT MOOSETRAILS IN THE MIST Gary Lawless

9   LAKE IN THE MOUNTAINS John McKeith

10   WILDERNESS LOST, WILDERNESS REGAINED Robert Kimber

15   IRIS Jon Luoma

16   WILDNESS AND WET Frank Graham, Jr.

21   LEOPARD FROG METAMORPHOSIS D. D. Tyler

22   NOT WILDERNESS Mitch Lansky

31   FOR THOSE WHO WOULD COMPROMISE THE FOREST Gary Lawless

33   MOOSE ON THE GREENVILLE ROAD Chris Ayres

35   DEBSCONEAGS Karin R. Tilberg

36   CONSERVATION THROUGH PRIVATE ACTION Kent W. Wommack

39   IF YOU LOVE THE LAND, OWN IT NOT! Charles FitzGerald

47   THE GOOD NEWS Gary Lawless

49   CLEARCUT Robert Shetterly

50   THE VIEW FROM MY SPRUCE Bernd Heinrich

53   CLOUD-CAPPED J. Thomas R. Higgins

54   DIRTY WORD Phyllis Austin

65   RED FOX IN SNOW   D. D. Tyler

66   GRAMP'S GIFT   Greg Shute

71   ST. JOHN RIVER   Bill Curtsinger

72   THOREAU IN THE MAINE WOODS   Robert M. Chute

74   NEVER LET GO THE DREAM   Garrett Conover

81   THE DANCE   Bunny McBride

89   LOOKING SOUTH FROM HAMLIN RIDGE ON KATAHDIN
Bill Silliker, Jr.

90   THE TRAIL NORTH   Bob Cummings

95   HIKING ON BIGELOW   Karin R. Tilberg

97   EAST TO BIGELOW   Margurite Robichaux

98   IF WE DON'T HAVE WILDERNESS. . . .   Jon Lund

103   PINE MARTEN   Jerry Stelmok

104   A FOREST RESERVE SYSTEM FOR MAINE
Malcolm L. Hunter, Jr.

107   THE HARRIER   Kate Barnes

109   BIRDS OF THE FOREST   Margaret Campbell

110   TREE   Susan Hand Shetterly

116   WILDERNESS IN TIME FUTURE   John Cole

121   LITTLE SPENCER MOUNTAIN   Jym St. Pierre

122   WILDNESS AND WILDERNESS   Lloyd C. Irland

129   LYNX AND GRAY JAY   Dean Bennett

130   CARVING WILDERNESS OUT OF CIVILIZATION
Dean Bennett

137   SONG FOR THE ALLAGASH   Alexandra S. B. Conover

139   BOREALIS   Franklin Burroughs

146   UPPER SOUTH BRANCH POND   Jon Luoma

148   COVER IMAGES

INTRODUCTION

Entering the barely penetrable basin on the northwest side of Katahdin is a wilderness homecoming. The view of steep granite walls, dog-hair evergreens, and dark, cold waters is at once breath-taking and scary, inspiring just the kind of electric reaction you might expect, even desire, in the most untamed, majestic landscape Maine has to offer. Or a climb up Old Speck Mountain in early morning darkness brings you into a disorienting, mysterious world of gray granite and gray fog. Then as the mists fade away, leaving you tiny and exposed, you see below you the emerging panorama of the Mahoosucs—fiercely enchanting and wild.

For many people, experiences like these are why they choose to live in Maine. Indeed, the very word "Maine" suggests opportunities to roam freely over a vast, wooded landscape and discover pockets of undisturbed beauty, to drift at dusk in a canoe on the mirror surface of a forest pond, to fall asleep at night beneath towering pines and a clear, star-flecked sky untainted by a synthetic glow. But over the past five decades, the impacts of industrial timber harvesting and the ever expanding network of logging roads in the state's wildlands have made it increasingly difficult to find the kinds of places that make these experiences possible.

Yet we know that Maine people care deeply about such places. They voice their support for wilderness areas in their testimony at legislative hearings, their written comments on agency management plans, their letters and op-ed pieces in newspapers, their responses to public opinion surveys and polls, and their generous contributions to conservation organizations and projects. But if that support is to bring about any action, it has to be orchestrated into a collective voice that will convey unequivocally to our leaders in conservation, business, and government that a solid public backing now exists for the creation and protection of some large wilderness reserves in Maine.

When we use the word "wilderness," we are not talking about landscapes that have never been touched by human hands. The lower elevations of Old Speck and much of Baxter State Park were at one time cutover lands. Now, they are examples of wilderness reclaimed, places where human beings have made a conscious decision to manage not for economic values but for values of the wild: peace, solitude, and the richness and beauty of flourishing plant and animal life that are possible only in deep forests where management is left largely to nature herself.

What we hoped to do in this book was bring together many voices that would speak for those values from a wide range of perspectives. We did not expect that every writer, artist, and photographer we invited to participate would share our particular view of what constituted wilderness, and as the contributions began coming in, we found that expectation confirmed. This book has its fair share of unabashed wilderness advocates calling for large, unroaded forest reserves in Maine where nature can rule. But you will find quite other views of wilderness as well. As one contributor wrote to us, "I don't think I can write about wilderness. I've never been there. I am a city boy who is thrilled by the 'wildness' of our backyard, a place where I have seen fisher, moose, fox, coyote and more, which is way wild enough for me. I've never wanted to paddle the Allagash. So I'm not the writer for your book, but thanks for asking."

But of course he was and is just right for this book, as are others who have written here not about big wilderness but about places close to home that evoke a sense of wilderness. Kate Barnes writes of "the harrier quartering / over the brown grass" on her farm. Frank Graham takes us into the wetlands along Tomah Stream in eastern Maine, a place not remote but, as he shows us, one teeming with wildlife. Even in our most domesticated landscapes, these writers remind us, wilderness should always be a presence. We should always have some access to wild places of adventure and enchantment, even though, as Frank

Graham says, they may "lie within sound of a busy highway." Life in Maine—life anywhere in Maine, north or south—has to have its quotient of wilderness, or it is not life in Maine.

So this book is all the richer for these differing views of wilderness. It is the richer, too, for the contributions that take on the thorny practical questions. It's all well and good to say how wonderful and important wilderness is; it's another matter to say just how large our designated wilderness lands should be, what their boundaries should be, and by what mechanisms and under what auspices—public, private, or a combination of the two—they should be protected. Maine Guide Garrett Conover insists we cling tenaciously to the dream of big wilderness and offers some suggestions about where it should be and who should manage it. Forestry consultant Lloyd Irland gives some hard thought to just how we might preserve wilderness in our present context, given present ownership patterns and the increasing demands of an ever growing population for forest products and recreational opportunities.

But no matter what poem or essay you read here, whether it is primarily political, historical, emotional, economic, or scientific in approach, and no matter which photograph or work of art you admire, it is clear that for each contributor to this volume wilderness matters. Each one knows how important it is for Maine's natural integrity, Maine's identity, Maine's soul, Maine's sanity, and—on a more prosaic level—for Maine's economy to have big, deep wilderness places you can go and get good and lost, places where the trees can grow big enough to qualify for the King's Arrow and then just fall down rather than be harvested for lumber.

In this book's first essay, Neil Rolde acknowledges the obstacles to wilderness preservation and designation but nonetheless urges us to "keep the banner of 'wilderness' flying if for no other reason than that it inspires us to the highest of heights in all of our conservation efforts." It is our hope that this book will not only keep the banner of wilderness flying but will also encourage discussion of how we can cultivate and nurture wilderness not only in thought but also in deed; for, we believe, Maine without some big reaches of designated wilderness and without wilderness interwoven into its settled lands is a Maine diminished, a Maine no longer Maine at all.

Consider this book, then, our attempt—and an attempt of the authors and artists represented here—to reclaim wilderness both as a word and as a reality on the land. We think it is time to raise a collective voice in praise of wilderness and all it means to Maine people—its enchantment and mystique, its place in our history, and its contribution to our cultural heritage. For the sake of the land's health and the health of the human spirit, it is time to speak out for wilderness.

Phyllis Austin
Dean Bennett
Robert Kimber

NEIL WELLIVER is a realist landscape painter of Maine's woods and waters. He lives on a farm in Lincolnville and has a cabin in the Allagash region. Many of his paintings in the '90s were of the Allagash and St. John River areas, and he has painted from canoe, snowshoes, or cross-country skis. A native of Millville, Pennsylvania, he is a graduate of the Philadephia Museum College of Art (1955) and Yale University (1955). He taught at Yale for almost a decade, was chairman of the University of Pennsylvania's Graduate School of Fine Arts, and has been professor emeritus at the graduate school since 1989. Dozens of galleries from coast to coast have shown Welliver's paintings, and many art museums have his works in their permanent collections.

St. John—Winter, 2000

Neil Welliver

Aquatint on Fabriano Tiepolo, 23 x 22 inches, sheet edition 40.
Created from two steel-faced copper plates using three colors.
Courtesy of Alexandre Gallery, New York, New York.

WILDERNESS

Neil Rolde

From the standpoint of Maine history, "wilderness" as a concept may be said to have had a checkered career. Among the Native Americans, it could be argued, there was no sense of wilderness as we conceive it, i.e., the absence of human presence. To the Indians, all nature was animate; rocks, trees, and mountains were sentient beings; animals and some humans were often interchangeable. Furthermore, there was no separation between "The People," which most tribes called themselves, and their natural surroundings.

The advent of Europeans brought much different ideas. The English Puritans who were to dominate Maine spoke of its vast forests as a "howling wilderness" and considered it an abode of Satan and his minions. Cutting the trees down, "letting in the light," was deemed a holy duty. They justified their taking of Indian land on the grounds that the Indians didn't work it; Indian men were "lazy," because all they did was hunt and fish, which in England were pastimes of the rich, not work. Of course, these new settlers were delighted to hunt and fish themselves, privileges denied them in England, activities that, in Maine, became a "right," and a doorway to an appreciation of the need for wildness, if not wilderness.

Maine was never conceived to be the immensely forested and unpopulated area it became. In need of money both before and after the American Revolution, the reigning government, which was the Massachusetts legislature or "General Court," as it is still called, divided up their "Eastern Lands" in Maine for sale, because the Commonwealth had no other major asset. The surveyors laid out townships of 23,000 acres that were supposed to become towns, whose populations would turn them into farms and centers of "civilization." In much of central and northern Maine, this transformation never happened. The land remained mostly as it was, even after it was sold to lumbermen and speculators. Indeed, since the Civil War, the forest acreage of the state has grown exponentially, as many marginal farms were abandoned.

The woods were not let alone, however. They were cut, grew back, and were cut again. Thus, we have the rather specious argument, used by some anti-environmentalists, that there is no real wilderness in Maine.

So what is real wilderness? I was struck recently by a passage in Harvard Professor Edward O. Wilson's 1994 book *Naturalist*, where the noted ecologist and world-class expert on ants writes: "But micro-wildernesses exist in a handful of soil or aqueous silt collected almost anywhere in the world. They at least are close to a pristine state and still unvisited. . . . A lifetime can be spent in a Magellanic voyage around the trunk of a single tree."

Wilson, the great champion of biodiversity, was expressing a feeling I had had several months before when, for the first time in my life, I had participated in an archaeological dig. Our quarry, as we sunk our trowels into the ground and sliced away, was human relics, arrowheads and pieces of pottery, but I found myself fascinated by the life we were uncovering as we went down layer by layer—unfamiliar worms and grubs and centipedish insects; and I actually did think: Here was a sort of wilderness under the turf we had removed that I had never been privy to. . . . Yet on a more familiar scale, when I decided to risk snorkeling in the frigid waters off that site in Brooklin, Maine, there was also the sense of wilderness I always feel when I'm gazing around underwater.

It wasn't just that I was the only person swimming. I have felt the same on snorkeling trips to coral reefs, where there might be several dozen people around me. I am in a natural element. The hand of man has only lightly touched these surroundings, if at all, even a short distance offshore. In Maine that day, I did not actually see any fish, but I was in a wonderland of undersea life and scenery just as soon as I put my mask in the water—the bright yellows and pinks of the granitic boulders, the contrasting green and red algae, the starfish, the urchins, the sand dollars on the bottom, the periwinkles on barnacled rocks, the beds everywhere of large, blue mussels—it was all undisturbed, carrying on as if this interloping observer from the world above was simply not in existence. Nor did I stay too long in that icy, albeit fascinating, environment.

What, then, of "wilderness," as some of the authors in this book would perhaps like to conceive it—vast tracts of untouched forests, pristine lakes, freely rushing rivers, wild mountains . . . room for the largest of roaming animals, no roads, maybe a few tracks for walkers and a water route for canoeists and kayakers.

Maine has such places, but are they enough? When The Nature Conservancy says it will make a reserve of 45,000 acres out of the 150,000 it bought on the upper St. John, does that gladden hearts or disappoint? Is there space for compromise as the natural world shrinks before the seemingly inexorable rise of the population of the species Homo sapiens?

In that same book, *Naturalist*, Edward O. Wilson speaks of "biophilia"—a term he coined to express that innate sense built into our species that draws us instinctively to the natural world, that makes us want to walk in the woods or go to the beach or camp out or fish or hunt or flee the city life if we can. "In Wildness is the preservation of the World" is Thoreau's much quoted and frankly (to me) enigmatic statement made after his exposure to the Maine Woods. Yet, whether we grasp his total meaning or not, it is an aphorism that has clearly touched a nerve down through the decades since he penned it and conceivably means more to us today than in his own day when the railroad and the steamboat and sawmills were the only big machinery with which he had to cope psychologically. The assault of automobiles, radios, TVs, airplanes, computers, you name it, on our daily senses certainly helps drive us to the quiet and incredible richness of a place deep within nature—for a respite—since a permanent home in such isolation is reserved for only a rare few who have the appropriate temperament.

The "deep ecologists" who would like us to go back to tribal living and turn all the world into wilderness are hardly being realistic. Will Americans give up hot showers permanently? And how do we organize 6 to 12 billion people into units of 100 or less?

Moreover, not all of us are "biophiliacs." Not any longer. Programmed into the makeup of some folks are those ancient fears of the dank, dark forest. "Little Red Riding Hood" is still a classic. Our own Stephen King a few years ago wrote *The Girl Who Loved Tom Gordon,* a horror story where the horror is a stretch of wilderness on the Maine-New Hampshire border in which a young girl gets lost. That is a conscious (or partly so) cultural kind of programming; deeper inside us, genetically placed through evolution, E. O. Wilson thinks, are phobias regarding certain inhabitants of the outdoors—snakes, rodents, spiders, etc.—that some of us can't stand, and Hollywood will even pick on birds and bees and turn them into deadly monsters scaring the beejeebies out of customers who actually pay to see this stuff.

Then, too, there are those who make a profit from not having wilderness. Theirs is a very conscious programming, although they probably like to go fly fishing or quail hunting. And the belief in the ideology of development can be genuine. I once had a professor at Yale who declaimed, apropos of T. S. Eliot, that "You don't write a poem about a wasteland. You take a bulldozer and create a civilization out of it." Even then—and this was in the '50s—we booed him. In any event, ambivalence on this subject of what we should leave wild is everywhere.

What is hopeful in this conundrum is that we have begun to recognize what we are doing to our planet. We are far from having stopped all harmful activity, but knowing that it is harmful is a start. The efforts to preserve important areas, even in Maine, are light years ahead of what they were when I first came to the state forty years ago. Organizations have formed; citizens have mobilized; money has been raised; land bought. Dozens of local "wildernesses" are being spared from the juggernaut of development pressure.

That we may not have wildernesses on the scale of days of yore is a disappointment, to be sure. That the Amazon is dwindling pains me, although I have never been there. Our triumphs may be on a minor scale: A plant saved from extinction because a human has been brave enough to scale down a Hawaiian cliff and pollinate it by hand is still a victory. A patch of jungle set aside in the Congo to protect rare simians is another win. A whole island in the Pacific and its surrounding reefs fenced off-bounds to exploitation. . . . It may not be enough or as much as we would like, but it is something.

We must keep the banner of "wilderness" flying if for no other reason than it inspires us to the highest of heights in all of our conservation efforts. If it proves to be an unattainable goal in every case, the progress the quest for it promotes is far from a losing cause. Plus there is also the knowledge gained by constant inquiry into the natural world—like E. O. Wilson's excitement about all those unknown critters in his microwildernesses. Scientists say there are still thousands of species of living things yet to be discovered, out there in the varied "wildernesses" that our touch has not yet reached or contaminated.

If we keep on striving to do the best we can by this beautiful "blue marble" planet of ours, we'll get it right yet.

NEIL ROLDE is the author of nine books, the latest, *The Interrupted Forest,* a history of the Maine Woods. He also has been involved in Maine politics and government, as an assistant to former Governor Kenneth Curtis, a member of the Maine house for sixteen years and a member of various commissions and task forces. He has served and continues to work on many non-profit organization boards. Rolde lives in York with his wife, Carla, and they have four daughters and seven grandchildren.

Nothing but moosetrails in the mist,
today's fog and wind,
trees against sky.
I want to disappear into cloud,
wander my way to sunlight,
follow the moose down
secret trails in the woods
to reach the places where the wolves
rest above the ridges, within us,
where the heart wanders, wild.

—Gary Lawless

GARY LAWLESS was born in Belfast and has lived in Maine ever since. He and his partner, Beth Leonard, live as caretakers at Chimney Farm, the Maine home of writers Henry Beston and Elizabeth Coatsworth. Gary is co-owner of Gulf of Maine Bookstore in Brunswick and editor/publisher of Blackberry Books. He is poetry editor of *Wild Earth* magazine and has published eleven collections of poems in the U. S. and three collections in Italy (including his book *Caribuddhism,* called *Caribudismo* in Italian!). He has given poetry readings and workshops in the U. S., Italy, Slovenia, Latvia, and Lithuania, all with a focus on loving and protecting the diversity of the natural world.

From my perch way up in the old fire tower on the top of Magalloway Mountain in New Hampshire, I was almost startled by the fiery beauty of the orange and red sunset over the Green Mountains of Vermont. A symphony of colors spread out before me, together reflecting from and embracing every cloud and lake and river in the scene.

At last the symphony was over, and the bold hues of red and orange faded to placid shades of amber. I glanced over to the east, not expecting to see anything that compared to the brilliance of the colors now slipping away. Night had nearly fallen on the Boundary Mountains of Maine, but if what I had seen to the west was the main performance, this was certainly the encore.

Not quite hidden among the steep slopes of blue was a small lake. I still do not know which lake it is, but it doesn't matter, really. I have wandered to that remote lake countless times in my imagination. Perhaps someday I will find that lake and sit on its shore or paddle its waters. Perhaps I will never find it and only imagine doing that.

JOHN MCKEITH has photographed the New England landscape for nearly two decades. His goal is to portray and celebrate the beauty, the wildness, and the delicacy of nature as it exists in the world around us and then share these remote places and wonderful moments with those who may never see them. John and his wife, Steffi, own the EarthImagery Gallery, featuring signed, limited edition prints of John's wildlife and landscape photography. His photographs are also regularly published by leading environmental organizations in their campaign and fund-raising publications.

LAKE IN THE MOUNTAINS
John McKeith

WILDERNESS LOST, WILDERNESS REGAINED

Robert Kimber

I can't tell you what anybody else's definition of wilderness is. There are probably as many definitions as there are people. But here's mine: Wilderness is big. It goes on for mile after mile, day after day. You can travel by foot or canoe for weeks at a time and see nothing but water and sky, tree and beast. Any evidence of human presence or works is so minuscule as to be inconsequential, maybe a trapper's tilt here, evidence of a fish camp there, lichen-covered rocks in an ancient tent ring that tells us native people camped on this site for millennia before European foot ever touched American soil. Wilderness goes on and on and on.

Here's another thing about wilderness: it's a European invention. When we Europeans arrived on this continent, we didn't find any roads, cities, theaters, churches, cow barns, tilled fields, or pasture fences. We were civilized people and needed these things to live, so we called this uncivilized landscape "wilderness" and set about recreating it in our own image. Native peoples had managed to live here for thousands of years without roads, churches, and pasture fences. They managed to find food, shelter, and clothing and create cultures here in the "wilderness," so for them it wasn't wilderness. It was simply home. As that superb western writer Reg Saner puts it: "Wilderness is all there was before there was any."

But once we Europeans had managed to convert most of the wilderness to civilization, some of us began to see that we had not vanquished an enemy but had crushed a friend. We began to see that no matter how wonderful the wonders were that we had worked on this continent—our skyscrapers, our suspension bridges, our steel mills, our ranches and farms and cities—none of them could stand comparison with the Grand Canyon, the Rocky Mountains, or, even, if you think about it, with any far more modest natural wonders, such as, say, our own Katahdin here in Maine or even just the hill back of my house in Temple.

Now that big wilderness is gone, we wish desperately that we had not squandered it so recklessly. We ache for those long vistas opening up before us, mile after mile, day after day. In Alaska and the Canadian North, some big wilderness is left. Down here in the lower forty-eight, we have only snippets and patches and rag-tag ends left over. Wilderness has gone from being all there was to a very scarce resource, especially here on our long-settled, heavily populated eastern seaboard.

So when we speak of wilderness now, those of us who advocate for it have no illusions. We are not talking about wilderness in the sense of all there was before there was any. That is the wilderness we have irrevocably lost. What we are talking about now is the wilderness we can regain by intent and design, wilderness as a management category. Because "the wilderness" is gone, we now have to designate "a wilderness" here and "a wilderness" there. "A wilderness" now is a tract of land we all agree to manage for its wilderness character, for peace, quiet, and solitude, a place where we allow plants and animals to live out their life cycles with as little human interference as possible. In short, if we are going to have wilderness in our settled regions, wilderness will have to be artificial. We will have to grow wilderness the way we grow peas and carrots. We will have to cultivate wilderness.

But surely, you will object, "cultivating wilderness" has to be a contradiction in terms, a prime example of oxymoron if ever there was one. Wilderness is at one end of the scale; cultivation is at the other. What is wild is not cultivated; what is cultivated is not wild; and never the twain shall meet. That is, I'm convinced, an outdated notion. Or, rather, it is a notion that was never correct in the first place. Thoreau's dictum "In Wildness is the preservation of the World" is all too familiar. Much less familiar and quoted much less often but—it seems to me vastly more important in our present context—is Wendell Berry's corollary to that dictum: "In human culture is the preservation of wildness." Any culture worth its salt will preserve wildness and wilderness because it knows that the richness and diversity wilderness provides is essential to ecological health, which is in turn essential to human physical, mental, and social health. Wildness is the wild card that makes an otherwise losing hand a winning one. As Michael Pollan points out in *The Botany of Desire*, if the Irish had not become totally dependent on one kind of potato, the Lumper, but had, like the Incas in the potato's Andean homeland, grown a variety of potatoes that were constantly crossing with wild varieties, the potato blight that struck Ireland in the 1840s could not have destroyed the entire Irish potato crop. Clearly, the more resilient and ultimately the more successful culture is the one that seasons its domestic life with substantial infusions of the wild.

We preserve our artistic heritage in museums, and so our designated wildernesses will have to be living museums in which we preserve our wild natural heritage. But, you may again object, isn't that hopelessly phony? What kind of "wilderness experience" can anyone have in a hothouse wilderness? A pretty darned good one, I'd say. Is the *Mona Lisa* any less beautiful now that it hangs in the Louvre and not in some duke's drawing room? Is Katahdin any less grand, lovely, and imposing because it is now in a "park"? I've spent enough time in the patches of wilderness still left in Maine, both designated and undesignated ones, to know there's nothing phony about that experience. The thrill of coming on a patch of ancient trees where I sink nearly knee deep in the mossy cushion underneath them is no less a thrill for the knowledge that this may be the only patch of old growth for miles around. I may wish for more land like this, but the scarcity of it hardly detracts from the experience of it.

Wendell Berry has also remarked that every farm needs a sacred grove, a place where no work is ever done, a place within ten minutes walk of the back door where we can always go and see (or at least begin to imagine) what the world was like before we humans ever touched hand to it. Designated wilderness areas have to be the sacred groves of our domesticated world. We know that wilderness matters to us. We have the testimony of poets, philosophers, scientists, nomads, ridgerunners, and bushwhackers down through the ages. We know, as Aldo Leopold wrote so many years ago, that wilderness is that "single starting-point, to which man returns again and again to organize yet another search for a durable scale of values."

Maine has priceless natural areas that merit the protection of wilderness designation. It is time for men and women of good-will to put their heads together and devise the means—political, economic, and administrative—to secure that protection.

ROBERT KIMBER has spent a fair amount of his adult life running around in the Maine Woods. He has written for *Audubon, Field & Stream,* and a number of other magazines. His books include *A Canoeist's Sketchbook, Upcountry: Reflections from a Rural Life,* and, most recently, *Living Wild and Domestic: The Education of a Hunter-Gardener.* Kimber and his wife, Rita, have collaborated on upward of forty translations from the German. The Kimbers lives on an old farm in Temple.

IRIS

Jon Luoma

JON LUOMA is an artist and illustrator who lives in Alna. He has served on the boards of local land trusts, on the Allagash Wilderness Waterway advisory committee and is part of the current effort to restore the Allagash to federal Wild and Scenic River standards of "generally inaccessible except by trail." In 1998 he illustrated a limited letterpress editon of Thoreau's *The Maine Woods.* The original drawings are in the Portland Museum of Art.

Wildness and Wet

Frank Graham, Jr.

A friend of mine who combines a passion for wilderness with a quirky sense of humor refers to his remote Edens as realms "where the hand of man has never set foot." All of us who treasure the outdoors need a secret place, though it may even lie within sound of a busy highway. (From his Walden, remember, Thoreau could hear the bellow of a distant locomotive.) But the surroundings themselves must create an aura of solitude. A place of adventure, if you will, or of enchantment, or perhaps simply a plot of land where we can go to be alone for a while. For some of us, this retreat is a cathedral-like forest. For others, it is a mountain top, or a desert, or a flowery meadow.

I am drawn to the wet places of the earth. Water is the stuff of life, and nowhere can one find a more marvelous hodgepodge of wild plants and animals than in the bogs, bayous, deltas, mangrove islands, and cypress swamps of our planet. Gerard Manley Hopkins, that poet of godly things, understood this passion. It shines through in these lines:

> What would the world be, once bereft
> Of wet and of wildness? Let them be left,
> O let them be left, wildness and wet;
> Long live the weeds and the wilderness yet.

On the contrary, most of our ancestors perceived in the wildness and wet a domain of horror. Beowulf's Grendel emerged at night from his lair in the dank mere to devour the locals, and Sherlock Holmes's Great Grimpen Mire was home to bloodcurdling yowls and a ravening hound. Even today, our exhilaration in entering a swamp or a bog is tinged with a faint but delicious whiff of danger.

Memory takes me back to one of my wild places in eastern Maine, the wetlands along Tomah Stream. My friend Cassie Gibbs of the University of Maine took me there and gave me an illustration of that illusion of risk brought on by creatures of the marsh. It seems that a couple of tourists, driving into Maine from New Brunswick on Route 6, stopped in Codyville Plantation to admire the stream, which passes under a bridge there and winds away through a wet meadow into the distance. A moment later, the couple beat a hasty retreat, pursued as they thought by a swirling cloud of enormous "mosquitoes" that had materialized out of the wetland.

"Those people stopped at a nearby store and made it sound as if they had narrowly escaped being eaten alive," Cassie told me. "But what they saw was a big mating swarm of perfectly harmless insects—Tomah mayflies."

Gibbs, an aquatic entomologist for many years at the university, is keenly aware of the variety of life nourished by Tomah Stream. In 1978 she rediscovered for science the insect now called the Tomah mayfly. Despite her frequent encounters there with voracious black flies, driving rains, and Arctic winds, she can think of no good reason to search out spectacular scenery in far-away climes. Tomah Stream contains a universe of her beloved aquatic insects thriving among a background of wetland plants and animals.

The tale of the map is prosaic enough: the stream flows out of Tomah Lake in eastern Maine, winds for twenty miles or so through forest-lined marshes, and northeast of Princeton enters Grand Falls Lake, which in turn empties into the St. Croix River. The area has been logged for over a century. Much of the Tomah Flowage, which includes the stream and the land it drains, has been owned by a paper company, which now lets Maine's Department of Inland Fisheries and Wildlife manage it.

But there is another element here. Tomah Stream is a protean element in the landscape, a pseudo-organism periodically swelling and overflowing the unique sedge marsh it has created and sustains, then retiring again into its accustomed course. This surge of water, which gathers in spring and overspreads the bordering sedges to a depth of a foot or more, prevents shrubs and trees from advancing into the marsh; the water's partial retreat in summer enables Tomah's rich community of plants and animals to carry on the cycles of their lives.

Sedges set the tone in the marsh. The keystone species of this aquatic family at Tomah is the tussock sedge, whose dead leaves annually form thick, tangled mounds above water or dense mats beneath the surface and provide habitat for a variety of wildlife.

"The nymph of the Tomah mayfly becomes a predator in spring, feeding on the nymphs of smaller mayflies," Cassie said, "and those prey animals depend for food on detritus from the decaying sedges. Sedges give all the aquatic insects hiding places from the fish that follow the water out onto the flood plain."

Mayflies form a basic link in the food chains of streams and ponds, being best known as food (and bait) for freshwater fish. The Tomah mayfly was named *Siphlonisca aerodromia* early in this century because the prominent flanges on its abdomen reminded naturalists of the wings of an "aerodrome," originally a synonym for airplane. (Like most other biological lowlife, it was not dignified by a vernacular name.) The mayfly was known only from New York's Sacandaga River. When that river was dammed in the 1930s, the mayfly disappeared, and scientists thought it extinct. Since Cassie Gibbs rediscovered it along Tomah Stream, she has found it in a number of other wetlands in Maine, and other biologists have recorded it from eastern Canada.

But Tomah Flowage, where the insect finds both abundant habitat and plenty of food, seems to have the largest numbers. This mayfly's presence is almost a certification of the wildness of its habitat.

"Thousands of dams have been built in the state—for mills, water storage, and transporting timber—from colonial times to the present," Cassie explained. "The dams greatly modified Maine's river systems and drastically reduced their normal patterns of seasonal flow. Good habitat gets wiped out."

Ironically, the nature of human exploitation in the Tomah Flowage permitted the mayfly's survival there. Loggers dammed the stream during the nineteenth century to create storage areas for their logs. But in spring they broke the dams to float the logs to mills, bringing about a pattern that mimicked the natural cycle of events that has now been restored—a surge of water after ice-out that flooded the meadows and then receded. The mayfly probably didn't notice the difference!

During a recent September, before the first frost, I went back to Tomah alone. The stream coiled through the sedges, which rose like walls on either side. But the meadow is only a phantasm of dry land. As I walked into it, I would put one booted foot high and dry on a tussock, while the other remained in several inches of water. There were flashes of color among the dark brown stems of sedges and grasses—cardinal flowers still blooming among the asters and goldenrods, and the blunt rosy spikes of water smartweed emergent in the shallows. A bald eagle dipped and glided among the tips of spruces across the meadow.

There was no hint of a world beyond. I could hear the slap of a beaver's tail, the harsh *chack* of a yellowthroat, the constant whirr of cicadas. No animal life was visible close to me, but when I passed a sweepnet through the vegetation, the cloth came alive with scurrying or flitting forms—crane flies, leafhoppers, stinkbugs, crab spiders, and tiny black chalcid wasps. Then out of the dusk a large insect appeared, flying straight toward me, and I took pleasure in imagining it to be one of Cassie Gibbs's mayflies.

The only vestiges of *Siphlonisca aerodroma* in Tomah Stream, I knew, were now bedded down as eggs, waiting to hatch next year into a fleeting new generation. The dragonfly, for that's what the insect was, swept past me. But the awareness of exhilarating confrontation, of another world around me that once struck terror into the human heart, was certainly consistent with my experience in Maine's watery wilderness.

FRANK GRAHAM, JR., resides in Milbridge and has been a field editor of *Audubon* magazine since 1969. He is the author of *Since Silent Spring, The Adirondack Park, Where the Place Called Morning Lies, Maine's Dominion: The Story of Conservation in America, The Audubon Ark,* and more.

Leopard Frog Metamorphosis

Rana pipiens

D. D. Tyler

To me, the gold worn in brilliant flecks by leopard frog tadpoles is more valuable than the bankable gold of commerce, just as the richness of an intact wilderness far exceeds any wealth created by its dismantling.

D. D. TYLER is an artist of natural history, born and raised in Kansas. Her illustration career began in the early 1970s at *Maine Times* and was followed by illustration of fourteen books, paintings and the formation of Tyler Publishing. In 1989 Tyler began creating designs for t-shirts printed by Liberty Graphics, producing over a hundred designs to date. She has traveled widely and enjoys observing nature in the field as well as through extensive research. Tyler lives in a secret location in Hallowell with her husband, Hank. They have two grown children, Zachary and Kate.

Not Wilderness

Mitch Lansky

I've traveled extensively in what is called "wilderness" in Maine. I've hiked on the Appalachian Trail, paddled down (or since it is North, is it up?) the Allagash, and cross-country skied the entire length of Baxter State Park. While the physical landscapes of mountains and rivers have been awe-inspiring, most of the forests have not. On the trail and on the river, I've sometimes seen a bit too much light pouring in a few hundred feet away. I've seen some woodlots in better shape than much of the forest in Baxter State Park. Something inside me has an urge to see nature fully expressed, and the "wilderness" I've seen in Maine, except for tiny pockets of old growth, just doesn't satisfy that urge.

Unlike Alaska, where huge, wild landscapes that were never exploited for timber are called "wilderness" and protected from development or cutting, "wilderness" in the East is made up of previously managed landscapes where cutting and clearing is no longer allowed. Before it was bought by Percival Baxter (and even, in some cases, after his purchase), most of Baxter State Park was either cut or burned or both. There is even an area in the park, New City, where I found remnants from abandoned farms. When I hiked on parts of the Appalachian Trail in southern New England, I went over many a stone wall in the middle of the forest.

In the past, Maine's unmanaged (or very minimally managed) forest land was the landscape context, and human settlements and intensively managed lands were a content—a black dot in a white circle. Now, a managed landscape is the context, and unmanaged lands are a content—a white dot in a black circle.

According to the latest state forest inventory, "reserved" forest comprises only around 1.5 percent of Maine's acreage.

Society has changed its concepts of the white and black dots—the yin and yang of nature and the made/managed world. Currently, nature is seen as a resource, serving the economy. If there is to be wilderness, it has to pay its way—it needs to be a form of development. Some wilderness proponents assure the public that wilderness does create jobs and improve the economy, as if that is what is needed for justification. As if the crowds needed to produce the biggest economic return are a good thing.

"Wilderness," like God, freedom, and love, means different things to different people. Often, when arguing about these concepts, people are talking past each other because they are not talking about the same things. They are thinking about different scales, different uses, different managers, and different beneficiaries. How people perceive the meaning of "wilderness" impacts how they treat the land.

To the first European settlers, Maine's forest was a "wilderness" because it was untamed. It was "wild"—growing for itself and not for man. It was also somewhat frightening, if not, perhaps, somewhat evil, with large, dangerous animals and "wild" Indians. But it did have a wealth of resources ready to be exploited—furs and timber.

The modern perspective of "wilderness," for some, is a green backdrop for recreation adventures. It is a landscape that has no traces of permanent human habitations or factories or stores—though there can be huts or campsites. Motorized vehicles are not permitted in this "wilderness," although I do note that there is one type of camper/trailer called "Wilderness." Apparently, some people see wilderness as something that can be attached to a car.

With the official version of "wilderness," however, people are visitors, not residents. It is a place for nature, as the cities and suburbs are a place for people. Ironically, the original "wilderness" found by the first settlers from Europe, was one that *did* have Native American residents who had tribal, clan, and family hunting territories. These First Peoples lived in the woods seasonally, and used plants and animals for food, shelter, medicine, and tools.

The native languages of Maine have no words for "wilderness." More than a decade ago, I asked a Penobscot friend what the word for "forest" was in Penobscot. I wanted to contrast that to our concepts of the "industrial forest" and "wilderness." Since there was only one living person left who was still fluent in the language, Madeline Shay, he went to her and asked. Next time I saw him, he gave an answer, which sounded to me like "kcheegook." I asked what that meant literally. Once again, he went to Madeline for the answer. When next I saw him, he told me that she said "kcheegook" referred to the place, where, when in a camp, you go when you have to relieve yourself.

When Henry David Thoreau first proposed a park for Maine, his concept was not for a people-free landscape. Instead, he envisioned a landscape "in which bear and panther, and some even of the hunter race, may still exist, and not be 'civilized' off the face of the earth." Such a concept is foreign to current thinking about wilderness, perhaps because more recent "traditional uses" involve motor vehicles and guns, rather than canoes and bows and arrows.

The exclusion of people in parks, however, has sometimes had insidious results in Third World nations. Native peoples have been excluded from their subsistence hunting and foraging lands so that tourists from the industrialized nations can view the wildlife. One sanctuary ranger in Thailand observed that "We have our ancestors to blame for our predicament. If they had not protected these forests over so many centuries, we would not be threatened with eviction today."

To others, wilderness is an unmanaged wasteland. It is not producing anything useful. It is a good place to site dumps or hold military exercises. Remote recreation is a single use that precludes all other uses, whereas logging (producing goods that everyone, everyone, everyone needs) allows "multiple uses." Multiple uses are "obviously" of greater benefit to society than a single use.

Maine has come up with a compromise—corridors and buffers around the Appalachian Trail and the Allagash where cutting is restricted, and working-forest easements over hundreds of thousands of acres, where timber harvesting can continue unabated, but development is restricted. Some enthusiastic literature about these easements actually refers to the land as "wilderness" that is being "preserved" or "protected," even though most of the forest can be roaded, clearcut, sprayed, and converted to softwood plantations.

A key argument of those favoring such compromises is that society cannot afford to take more land out of production. Indeed, the Land for Maine's Future Board has in its guidelines that: "LMF is prohibited by statute to acquire land for which the primary use value has been or will be commercially harvested or harvestable forest land. This does not prohibit the acquisition of conservation easements on working forest lands which allow for timber production while securing public access and the conservation of other natural resource values."

Part of the logic behind such policies is that we "need" to meet projected demands for timber products and paper. If any land is taken from production, the wood will have to come from either more intensively managed land in Maine or from somewhere else. That "somewhere else" might be another country with fewer environmental protections, so "protecting" land here could cause an even worse impact to another region. From this "environmental paradox" we end up with the dictum that if we think globally, we have to cut locally.

A new concept has entered the debate: biodiversity. Some environmentalists are arguing we need wilderness preserves to protect the full range of species. Often the debate centers around large, "charismatic megafauna," such as wolves, cougar, caribou, or lynx. Some wildlife biologists, however, have pointed out that there are managed forests and developed regions in North America that support these species, without the need for wilderness. Actually, the species most at risk from continued cutting are very uncharismatic lichens, mosses, fungi, and insects, which can survive in fairly small areas. At least temporarily. There is not, currently, a big constituency advocating for lichens or fungi. It is easier to rally behind something big and furry than something small and slimy.

Biodiversity, however, does not just refer to species—it also refers to ecosystems. What is lacking in the East are complete ecosystems with all the habitats capable of supporting viable populations of all the native species over time. While the charismatic megafauna may not require wilderness to survive, wilderness ecosystems require these animals to be complete.

"Over time" implies change. Wind, fire, insects, and disease produce disturbances that change the structure and species ratios of stands and landscapes. The protected landscape has to be big enough, therefore to incorporate such disturbances without losing either habitats or species.

Reconstructions of the presettlement forest indicate that stands with trees hundreds of years old were the rule, rather than the exception as they are now. When there were large fires or windthrow, biological legacies that survived within the disturbance and the vast older forests outside the disturbance ensured that over time, habitats could recover and species recolonize. Full recolonization of logged habitats does not occur, however, if rotations are too short for habitat recovery and there are no refugia (or sources of species for recolonization) near enough. Indeed, the more intense the management (such as whole-tree clearcuts) the longer it takes to recover. Yet, ironically, it is with such heavily cut stands that some landowners are planning for the shortest rotations.

Even if we cease all logging, we cannot go back to the presettlement forests of hundreds of years ago that had these more "complete" ecosystems. Species, such as wolves, caribou, and cougar have been extirpated from Maine. Other species, such as passenger pigeons, will never return—they are extinct. There are new species, such as the Gypsy moth, that have come in and do not seem to want to go away. The climate has changed, and will continue to change, perhaps partly induced by human consumption of fossil fuels. And we have introduced toxins over the landscape—from pesticides to heavy metals to acid precipitation—that are having an impact on soil, fish, and ecosystem health. One does not have to cut a forest to change it.

Because our forests are no longer "virgin," that does not mean they have to forever be subject to rape. While we cannot go back to what was, we can, to some degree, partly recover forests to have more old-growth characteristics. Perhaps some of the extirpated species could return or be reintroduced as the landscape recovers. We have examples in the Adirondacks that such recoveries are possible, but they are certainly not instant. The logging that preceded the creation of the Adirondacks a century ago was far less intense than the logging of today. Recovery in parts of Maine will take much longer.

Beauty strips and management as usual are not sufficient to protect biodiversity for the long term. Some have proposed setting up small reserves that protect samples of all ecosystem types. The success of these smaller reserves, however, depends on how the land is managed around it. Intensive management, for example, could isolate the reserves as fragments. The current policies for ecological reserves and for purchasing public lands, even at their best, could not, over the long run protect biodiversity— unless landowners spontaneously decided to act like Percival Baxter and set up their own large reserves and model forests. Given the current mix of landowners, this seems unlikely in the short run.

More naturalistic management could buffer and extend the benefits of the reserves. Setting up a reserve system should not be seen as an either/or issue of lichens against loggers. We need a forest policy that sets up ecological reserves *and* improves forest practices *and* improves the viability of industry *and* strengthens local communities. It is entirely possible to cut fewer acres, but generate more value and create more jobs if we have a sensible forest policy.

Rewilding formerly managed landscapes takes time, perhaps hundreds of years. Calling a newly "protected" landscape a "wilderness" does not immediately erase the roads, create old growth or restore extirpated species. Parts of the forest, converted to large areas of balsam fir, will be susceptible to increased intensity, frequency, and extent of disturbances, such as the spruce budworm, for a long time, unless there is management to reverse such structures.

Which brings us to the key point of this essay—the value of wilderness depends on what is *not* wilderness. Outside the border of any wilderness is a landscape dedicated to serving perceived needs of an economy that must grow indefinitely into the future. The environmental paradox, where protecting land in Maine could lead to more destruction globally, is based on this ever growing demand as a constant, and nature as the variable. Those who posit this line of thinking do not carry it far enough—for a thousand years, for example. Projecting our economy a thousand years ahead leads to totally absurd situations— where we have to expand our industries into outer space, because there would be no space left on Earth.

If we really want a "wilderness" that functions to protect biodiversity for thousands of years, we will not succeed by cordoning off areas on the map to create nature museums, and assuming that everywhere else can be exploited to the full extent indefinitely. Nature does not start and stop by human dictate. It is all around us and within us. It is in the cities and suburbs. It is our life support, not a mere economic resource. We need to bring more wildness home, to where we live.

The idea that there is not sufficient land for wilderness is based on the assumption that it is okay for Americans to consume more than twice the forest products per capita as Europeans and six times greater than the world average. We are justified, under this line of thinking, to consume not only our forest resources, but those of other nations, if ours prove insufficient. There is another assumption worth examining—that it is okay to create communities that are so unfulfilling that people need to travel thousands of miles, towing along expensive, synthetic clothing and equipment, just to see and experience a "natural" landscape.

Unless we include our global consumption society in the debate, discussions about how much, if any, of "wilderness" we could have or can "afford" are absurd. We can not have a society that has ever growing resource needs in a world of limited resources. Words like "enough" need to enter into our vocabulary.

In *Beyond the Beauty Strip*, I wrote:
Maintaining wilderness implies restraint—restraint from exploiting or destroying every last acre of remaining forest. There are limits to the expansion of exploitive

management and forest conversion because there are limits to forests. At some point society must choose if it will live within these limits in a sustainable way or if it will continue expanding its industrial capacity until the resource capacity shrinks to nothing. Allowing the existence of wilderness may mean reaching the limits to growth sooner, but exploiting wilderness does not mean avoiding those limits. A society living within limits and maintaining wilderness would be richer than a society living within limits with no wilderness. As Thoreau once said, 'A man is rich in proportion to the number of things he can afford to leave alone.'

Although Maine's Native Americans may not have had a word that corresponds to our concept of "wilderness," they did have the tradition of the vision quest. The vision quester leaves the cocoon of family, village, and society and goes alone to a remote and wild spot, seeking identity, inspiration, power, or guidance. There he fasts and waits. The vision quester, in such a remote location, is not shielded from nature—including the wind and rain, the black flies and mosquitoes, or the wolves and mountain lions—by technology or social distractions. The quester becomes a very small dot in a very big circle—it is a frightening and humbling experience. This tradition of entering the wilderness for inspiration is also shared by Judeo-Christians. Moses went to the mountain and Jesus to the desert for their visions.

The Romantic Poets of nineteenth-century England felt the loss of that experience of wild, untamed nature. Wordsworth wrote, "Getting and spending we lay waste our powers, little we see in nature that's ours. We have given our hearts away, a sordid boon." In another poem he wrote, "To her sweet works did Nature link, the human soul which through me ran, and much it grieved my heart to think what man has made of man."

We live in a society where the dot thinks that it is the circle. Most of nature is tamed for the benefit of man. We even call Maine's woods a "working forest." In losing the wildness, we not only lose part of our "souls," we also threaten the stability of the man-made systems we are creating. Anthropologist Roy

Rappaport warned that "To regulate a general system such as a society or a forest in accordance with the narrow purposes of one of its sub-systems, such as a business firm or an industry . . . is to narrow the range of conditions under which the general system can survive."

English poet Gerard Manly Hopkins saw the same violence from the taming of nature that Wordsworth saw:

Why do men then now not reck His rod?
Generations have trod, have trod, have trod;
And all is seared with trade; bleared, smeared with toil;
And bears man's smudge, and shares man's smell; the soil
Is bare now, nor can foot feel being shod.

But he saw hope of renewal in this destruction:

And for all this, nature is never spent;
There lives the dearest freshness deep down things.

Even though much of Maine's forest has been "tamed," there is a capacity for rewilding. This is something to encourage and celebrate. We need complete, functioning ecosystems so we do not lose that which has sustained us. We need wilderness for our souls to be whole and complete. As Hopkins said in another poem:

What would the world be, once bereft
Of wet and of wildness? Let them be left,
O let them be left, wildness and wet;
Long live the weeds and the wilderness yet!

MITCH LANSKY is the author of *Low-Impact Forestry: Forestry As If the Future Mattered* and *Beyond the Beauty Strip: Saving What's Left of Our Forests*. He has also contributed to several other books. He is a founder of the Maine Low-Impact Forestry Project, a writer for the *Northern Forest Forum* and contributor to *Atlantic Forestry Review*. He has been on various government committees and task forces. A graduate of the University of Pennsylvania, Lansky is a long-term resident of Wytopitlock, a small forest-based community in northern Maine.

For Those Who Would Compromise
the Forest

the spirits of the lost trees,
the spirits of the plants,
the moss spirits, the rock spirits
consign you to a hell of
no birds, a dry spare hell where
your name will not be known—
you will be known as desolation,
ruiner of planets, the lonely soul who
lives without the friendship of life,
without the solace of species—
the ghosts of those you have
pushed aside will follow you as
you move toward dryness, dust
and empty skies—
surely goodness and mercy will
leave your wretched life untouched
as you dwell forever in
a land without life,
trying to remember the sound
of birds, the sound of wind,
the sound of your own heart,
beating.

       —Gary Lawless

Gary Lawless's bio is on page 7.

Moose on the Greenville Road

Chris Ayres

Wilderness is within us all—each of us. We mirror wilderness. Wilderness mirrors us. Without wilderness, we lose sight of our essential selves and are lost.

CHRISTOPHER AYRES has been a newspaper, magazine, and commercial photographer in Maine for many years. He was chief photographer at the *Maine Times* for over ten years. While there, he photographed most of Maine's natural, social, and political life. Ayres is widely known for his nature and landscape photography, doing work for nearly every major environmental and conservation organization in Maine. He is a founding member and participant in the popular "10 x 10" yearly art sale of works by ten Maine artists. His photos appeared in the book *Gulls*. He is a graduate of the University of Pennsylvania and has a master's degree in photography from the Institute of Design at the Illinois Institute of Technology in Chicago. He has lived in Maine since 1970 and is married with two children ages fifteen and twelve.

KARIN R. TILBERG currently serves as the deputy commissioner of the Department of Conservation. Previously, she served as the Maine director and interim executive director for the Northern Forest Alliance. During her tenure with the Alliance, she worked to promote the NFA vision for conservation of wildlands, sustainable forestry, and healthy, diverse local economies in Maine. She is an attorney and has practiced in the area of conservation and environmental law for many years, representing lake associations, municipal planning boards, citizen groups, and non-profit organizations. She has also held the position of staff attorney and director of advocacy for Maine Audubon Society and taught at the University of Maine School of Law. She has served on the boards of directors for many organizations, ranging from the Maine League of Conservation Voters to Figures of Speech Theater. She has a degree in wildlife biology from the University of Vermont and her law degree from the University of Maine School of Law. She is an avid outdoors person.

DEBSCONEAG DREAMS

We paddle from the Deadwater
Into First Debsconeag Lake
The entrance defined like cupped hands
Long strands of river grass collect the sun

The water is so clear that I doubt its existence
Underneath are flawless images of boulders and leaves
I think of the grinding down of mountains and the passage of
    time
The fish under the canoe are of ancient lineage

I leave the worries behind
There is no phone
Only the chaotic wonder of lichen and moss on the ridges
The secretive caves of ice

We land on warm sand shocking with soft beauty
I enter the water then, and let my body cool
Mingle with the slow flowing movement
Of water, cycling through the eight Debsconeag lakes

Lovely, large mayfly—*Hexagenia*—emerge
Pulling against the surface membrane of the Lake
Strong and ponderous, born from the surrounding wildness
Their huge silhouette dark, mysterious, against the yielding
    light

They enter the night and flutter into my dreams
They are the hopeful stars in an endless blanket
So thick and textured that it presses down on me
As I lie on the beach of sand and become only this moment,
    this place

—Karin R. Tilberg, December 2002

CONSERVATION THROUGH PRIVATE ACTION

Kent W. Wommack

The history of land conservation in Maine is primarily one of individual vision and generosity. Unlike the rest of the country, Maine's greatest parks and wilderness areas were created not by state or federal decree but through private philanthropy and leadership. This personal generosity has helped to define our state and enrich our lives. Imagine Maine without Baxter State Park, Acadia National Park, or Wolfe Neck State Park—all purchased and then donated to the public by visionary citizens.

Although few of us today could leave an individual legacy as large as Baxter State Park, together we can—by banding together and pooling our resources—acquire and protect places like the St. John River, the Debsconeag Lakes wilderness area, and Maine's most pristine coastal islands.

When The Nature Conservancy purchased 185,000 acres along the upper St. John River in 1998, it created a chance to preserve the best wilderness river east of the Mississippi. But turning this dream into a reality required $35 million, a fund raising goal many times larger than any previous non-college capital campaign in Maine history.

Yet within two years thousands of Maine people, year-round and seasonal, had donated the necessary funds for this acquisition. In many cases, individuals and families contributed ten times what they had ever donated to a charity before, and then called to thank me for "giving them the opportunity to be part of this project."

At first, these phone calls left me speechless. After making sacrificial financial contributions to help us save a corner of the northern forest—woods, lakes, and streams that most of these donors would never visit, and which would never bear their name—they were calling me to say thanks for asking them to contribute?

But I came to realize these sentiments reflect a deeply rooted desire of most people to leave the world a better place than they found it—to give something back for the benefit of future generations. Having grown up, recreated or worked in the great outdoors, most Mainers cherish the state's wild lands and natural areas. As Percival Baxter himself noted, all of Man's monuments and buildings will crumble over time, but Mount Katahdin will always be the mountain of the people of Maine.

Of course, the reasons people value these wilderness areas vary. Large natural areas provide refuge for plant and animal species that cannot survive in our sprawling suburbs, fields, and managed woodlots. They serve as baseline monitoring sites, which can help us understand and better manage the rest of the landscape. Some people believe it is our moral duty to preserve and protect that which God has given us; others simply want to protect a part of the world where they have found peace, wonder, and mystery—or experienced the thrill of sighting a bull moose or ruffed grouse.

Whatever motivates Maine people to treasure these wild places, they will not remain that way without conscious action. When polled on their vision for Maine, residents consistently say they want to protect more wilderness areas, a sentiment borne out in their personal generosity to private land conservation efforts throughout the state. In recent years, both state and federal programs have become more active in saving Maine lands, and these programs will become even more important in the future. It is essential that everyone who values Maine's uniqueness work together to preserve it.

So I invite each of you to join in this noble effort. Think about what kind of a state you want to leave for your children, and what special parts of Maine you want them to know as you do. Talk to your neighbors, join your local land trust, and contribute what you can to save a place you love. Future generations may not know precisely who preserved that spot, but they will cherish it just as we do Baxter or Acadia. I can think of no greater gift for our children, our grandchildren, or for Maine, forever.

KENT WOMMACK is executive director of The Nature Conservancy's 12,000-member Maine Chapter and a vice president of the worldwide Nature Conservancy. A graduate of Colby College and Yale School of Forestry and Environmental Studies, he joined the Conservancy in 1982 as an intern and served as director of land protection and as associate director before becoming executive director in 1991. He is responsible for the protection of nearly 600,000 acres of Maine's most important habitats, including the largest single land conservation purchase in the state's history—185,000 acres along the St. John River. Under Wommack's leadership, the Conservancy in Maine has received The Nature Conservancy's Outstanding Program of the Year Award three times in the last dozen years. *Downeast* magazine awarded its Environmentalist of the Year Award to the Conservancy's Maine Chapter in 1989 and to Wommack personally in 1999. In 1997 he was awarded the Kenneth M. Curtis Leadership Award by the Maine Development Foundation. He is the husband of Gro Flatebo and the father of three children.

If You Love the Land, Own It Not!
A Brief Personal History of My Maine Career

Charles FitzGerald

In 1967 I bought a farm in Maine. East of Dover-Foxcroft, deep in the adjoining town of Atkinson, were 65 acres of fields and 450 acres more of forests, marshes, and streams known as the Hart Speed Place. Much of the land bordered Alder Stream, a navigable-by-canoe tributary, coursing through the township from the west, exiting in the northeast corner, and tumbling furiously into the Piscataquis River.

When I bought the Hart Speed Place, I didn't know about Alder Stream nor was I familiar with the lay of the land or its boundaries. I barely glanced at the small farmhouse, took a quick look at the Farmall H sitting in the barn, asked the broker if I would own as far as I could see, and the deal was done.

I was thirty-three years old, a school teacher and small business owner in New York City. I had no idea that I had just taken a wrong turn on the road to traditional success, wealth, and security and that the seed of a grand obsession was planted in me that would short-circuit my growing business career and keep me on the sharp edge of necessity for the next thirty years.

That I survived after skirting bankruptcy several times is a testament to my good luck and the forbearance of others who allowed me to recover—that and the fact that I am a born merchant, a trader, a master of yard sales, a collector of other people's junk which I convert to gold.

My training ground was New York City where, armed with my handtruck, I nightly prowled the sidewalks of Park Avenue, supplementing my $68-per-week teacher's income with what the wealthy residents threw away.

Today, I still enjoy being a merchant. I'm always ready to bargain and make a deal. I like displaying goods in large piles, making things in my wood products factory and, of course, I love watching customers walk out of my stores laden with birdhouses and puzzle toys.

I grow most of my own food. I use scrap wood to heat the places where I live and work. I generally have two or three fifteen-year-old cars in the yard. I keep parts cars and glean from junk piles. My 20-foot canoes are my yachts and I can't live without duct tape. Living this way, I have more available income, but I don't appreciate the traditional security-enhancing uses of money. I have none, nor do I desire any life insurance, stocks, bonds, savings accounts, or IRAs. One credit card is enough. I travel light and am always moving at high speed. To know where I am going, I have only to observe where I've been since that August day in 1967 when my life was decided for me.

So, having bought the farm, I became a resident of Maine. I have been an organic gardener since I was six years old, so it was great to get my hands into real soil again after all the years of living and working in the big city and growing tomatoes on rooftops. I turned over and planted plots of corn, wheat, sunflowers, and potatoes all over the landscape. I turned out pigs to graze, and with the help of amiable Beethoven, the bull, bred a herd of 200 polled Herefords. Pigs and beefers alike ran down the road like molasses, ravaging neighborhood front yards. I tried to build better fences, contoured the fields, and planted alfalfa to restore soil fertility. I also began to walk the boundaries of the land, wander the forests, slog in the swamps, canoe Alder Stream, and watch the seasons and the landscape changing.

I befriended local old-timers who had spent their lives living and working in the woods. Fortunately, they were tolerant of long-haired urban transplants and were willing to teach me what they knew. I hunted with Gus Page who found the largest white pine in Maine. I followed Harry Edgerly on his trap line, setting for beaver, my cross-country skis a poor substitute for his snowshoes. I walked the woods of Massardis with forester Pete Sawyer (of the Dunn heirs) who patiently described the trees he loved and how they grew. And I camped and fished every fall on the

West Branch of the Penobscot with Myron Smart, who taught me how to pole the 20-foot canoe he made for me and who, in his warm wall tent on cold September mornings, spellbound me with stories of his experiences in the North Woods.

How fortunate I was to know them, these old men of the woods. I didn't know then, as I do now, how privileged I was to hear their stories, which they so freely and gently handed down to me. I didn't know how, with their quietly spoken Maine twangs, they were forging in me an unbreakable connection, stronger than a boom chain, to the forests, streams, and lakes of Maine.

By 1972 I learned that there was no time left. The Maine Woods clear-cutting rampage was beginning. I floated down the North Branch and the West Branch of the Penobscot on the last log drives. Bulldozed roads were coming in from all directions. Township-sized clear-cuts appeared around Ragmuff Stream and stretched all the way to Chesuncook Lake. The whine of harvesters and the roar of skidders went on day and night as I tried to sleep in my tent on Big Island.

Even Baxter Park was threatened as the then attorney general of Maine tried to make a deal with Great Northern, giving away the cutting rights to Baxter's Scientific Forest Management Area (SFMA) in the northwestern region of the park. It was a rude awakening that even the bequest of Percival Baxter to the people of Maine was subject to the monumental power of the timber barons; that public officials in state government could not be counted on to protect Baxter's legacy;; and that the state was our biggest adversary—representing and caving to the power of the timber industry.

So began my first lawsuit—challenging the state's right to trade off Baxter Park's timber. And then many more costly lawsuits followed.

There were the spruce budworm wars—several legal challenges to the ongoing aerial spray program; a lawsuit to stop the commercial harvest of the blowdown in Baxter Park and a later one to stop the reckless clear-cutting going on in the SFMA of Baxter Park. In every case, the overwhelming power of the state stood squarely in the way. The state is still standing in the way today, but the forests of Maine are not.

The relatively unbroken forests, which I flew over many times during the spruce budworm spray program, have been mostly replaced by a jumble of bulldozed roads, clear-cuts, and scars of erosion. The forest as I knew it is gone. That is the sum total result of fighting the state for thirty years. There were some exceptions, but the old dictum, "you can't fight City Hall" has been true most of the time. I felt I had no choice but to challenge entrenched special interests, but I ended up wasting a lot of time and money. The state juggernaut easily absorbed the impact of our energy and flattened us.

During all those financially exhausting years of court battles I was, fortunately, doing other things. Exploring the forests, fields, and streams of Atkinson always restored my equanimity and resolve. Even so, much of the land around me was under the constant threat of sale, subdivision, and clear-cutting—first the clear-cutting and then the strip subdivisions, all perfectly legal under state law. Although on a smaller scale, the threat was as inevitable as it was in the North Woods, and it was in my own backyard.

By this time, I had learned that the diversity of my small piece of Maine would be degraded along with the adjoining lands if they were cutover, subdivided, and developed. Enlargement was the only solution—where nature could thrive without the intrusion of uncontrolled human activity. Since there were no effective state regulations, I decided to respond in the only way possible—not by hopeless court actions to stop the rampage, or by futile attempts to move a reluctant legislature, but by buying all the land I could bordering the home farm and Alder Stream.

Unlike the North Woods, these were not township-sized parcels. Since the early 1700s, Atkinson has been subdivided into pieces ranging from one-half acre to several hundred acres. Three hundred years of human settlement have changed the landscape to a checkerboard of old farms and wood lots, some still active while others have faded back into the forest. Old cellar holes, stone walls, and rusty horse-drawn cultivators attest to a thriving farming community which had, at its height, supported more than 2,000 inhabitants. Today 300 or so people remain, settled mostly along the main roads. Most of the back country farms and wood lots have meltedback into the landscape, boundaries indistinct, forest habitats reintegrated, as the spruce, white pines, and tamaracks recolonize the fields while white birches and maples grow up in old potato house foundations. Since the decline of community-based agriculture, nature has swiftly asserted herself and has busily started obliterating the evidence of human intervention.

Most of these old farms border and drain into Alder Stream, a watershed full of meandering water courses, wild meadows, marshes, and swamps, with old caribou trails still visible crossing the peat bogs. Alder Stream itself is the twisting strand connecting and defining a still relatively intact ecosystem.

I discovered my new metier. I became an "undeveloper." I set out to buy every piece of land I could, every wood lot, every farm, every subdivision, every cabin and house lot—a Humpty Dumptyan task, tracking down numerous owners, making offers, and raising money. Some were ready to sell at a reasonable price, others at a price more than the land was worth, and a few sold to me because they knew I wouldn't tear apart the forests they loved so well. Many weren't ready to sell at all or wanted to cut the land first and then sell it. Once purchased, you had to be able to carry the costs of holding the land, paying the annual taxes, and providing watchful stewardship. Since the land could not provide an income, selling off income-producing assets became my only means to buy it and maintain it. I slowly began to realize that I could start this project but not finish it—that it would not come to fruition in my lifetime.

My own asset inventory dropped from about twenty retail stores and fifteen salable properties in the early 1970s to my present three retail stores and three small buildings. In a year or so, there will be one remaining retail store to keep my hand in and plenty of time to go back to teaching. Coming full circle was not a smooth journey. There were times when I couldn't go it alone and almost lost it all.

In 1987 I departed from the script and took a big leap into space. I borrowed more than a million dollars from a good friend and negotiated an option to buy the Diamond Occidental lands from a French company. With sixty days to raise $27 million, I went underground and worked around the clock. The result? I barked up a lot of wrong trees and in the end, couldn't make the deadline. The time was too short and I was too inexperienced to accomplish "mission impossible." My ship was sinking and I desperately (and irrationally) borrowed another $200,000 for another 30-day option to purchase Namakanta township. Predictably, I sank to the bottom. I had the will but could not find the means. My money went off to France never to be seen again.

Problem is, it was borrowed money and I had a $1,200,000 debt to pay back with interest. I struggled to pay the interest for a few years in a declining economy and finally was unable to make the payments.

One day Frank Murch, the well-loved sheriff of Piscataquis County, arrived at the door with a handful of foreclosure summonses and a jar of fresh horseradish, hand-picked and pickled by himself. In the months that followed, as I savored his kind and piquant gift, I was reminded that the present and hope for the future are far more important than the past. Follow your passion, take the consequences, and move on!

The following years were tough slogging but my memories of that struggle are already dim. There was a lot of plodding from pillar to post trying to shore up my assets, but in the end, like toppling dominoes, buildings were foreclosed. I watched a $2-million property in Bangor go to the city for one dollar, because I was a few dollars short on my taxes. In those days, there was no mercy anywhere.

Foreclosure was imminent on the land in Atkinson, when, at the last moment, a wilderness trust which takes very seriously its mission to set aside wilderness, purchased a conservation easement on the land from which the lien was paid.

Meanwhile, my success at expanding the Atkinson preserve had been curtailed for many years. Long-awaited opportunities to purchase key corridors in the watershed passed by as timber cutting and subdivision became more rampant. It happened that a well-known timber baron began to cut a large tract along

Alder Stream, near where it tumbles into the Piscataquis River—a vital addition to the preserve. To my delight, he agreed to stop cutting and sell. There was no place to turn for money but turn, I did, and found a friend and associate who shares the dream and who, without hesitation, purchased the tract, and then another, also along Alder Stream, and yet another in the headwaters—hundreds of acres, neatly falling into place, making vital connections in the landscape.

At the same time, the wilderness trust negotiated for and purchased several other large parcels. The map of our ecosystem began to look more contiguous—more than 20 miles of Alder Stream protected with uplands, forests, and cedar swamps stretching south into Charleston, east to Milo, and west into Dover-Foxcroft.

Having tipped my canoe, I had found friends with the same convictions, who, with steadier vision than mine, took over for a while, righted my canoe, and sent me on downstream. I'm snubbin' my way down Alder Stream more carefully now. I'm back to picking up more pieces of the puzzle and our preserve is growing again. Today, 35 years later, almost a hundred pieces of land, from half an acre to 700 acres make up a land and water preserve of over 12,000 acres—still fragmented, but coming together, a work in progress.

What's the bottom line? Is our investment in land appreciating? Can we spin off some profits? Whoa! The parlance of business won't serve us well here. Closed corporate systems measure success from within. Unless they are socially driven to do so, most corporations do not evaluate such things as impacts on surrounding ecosystems.

So what are the benefits? To know the answer I have only to observe what has happened to the land since I began piecing it together.

Thirty-five years have passed, a blink of the eye, half a human lifetime. Each year as I enter and explore a portion of the forest, I find that I am on an endless and wondrous journey of discovery. This is not the land I knew when I bought it—it is a new land full of promise and surprises. Having added thirty five years of growth rings, the big trees are becoming giants of their species—old growth. Clear-cuts are becoming forests again and cold springs are welling up where there were none before. There are signs of wildlife everywhere and a growing sense of wildness and solitude.

Because the old boundaries and tote roads have melted away, I am frequently lost. I stumble into acres of tangled blowdowns and dead balsam fir. I feel no anxiety, only excitement at seeing with my own eyes the dynamic changes in forest succession where rotting, fallen trees are rebuilding diversity—where death in the forest is the beginning of life in the forest. I am walking in awe of Nature's mysterious power to regenerate life if she is allowed to do so. We need only to reduce the relentless human intrusion, watch, wait, and protect. Nature will do the rest.

There is no bottom line here, no goal line, no blueprint for permanence, no finality. Rather, there is change, renewal, increasing abundance and fecundity, and, finally, evolution.

Last year, in mid-March, I was cross-country skiing south of my Atkinson cabin trying to lay out a cross-country ski trail, running through tall pines, skirting a great cedar swamp, and then looping back to the north. Crossing an open, broad reach of frozen swamp, I came to a remote knoll of several acres which I had never seen before. The snow beneath the hemlocks was crisscrossed with bobcat tracks. The flattened snowpack on the top of the knoll showed where the cats surveyed their domain. I saw no cats and returned to my cabin as the sun was setting. There's no need for a ski trail into that wild, remote swamp. The cats will do just fine without me.

CHARLES FITZGERALD is a wood products manufacturer, store owner, and organic farmer from Atkinson. He is continually and actively involved in environmental issues, including forestry, aquaculture, land preservation, and wilderness. The proceeds from the operation of his various small businesses have gone into the purchase and protection of Maine land.

THE GOOD NEWS

Roads disappear, and the caribou wander through.
The beaver gets tired of it, reaches
through the ice, grabs
the trapper's feet,
pulls him down.
Wolves come back on their own,
circle the state house, howl at the sportswriters,
piss on the ATVs.
Trees grow everywhere.
The machines stop,
and the air is full of birdsong.

—Gary Lawless

GARY LAWLESS's bio can be found on page 7.

CLEARCUT

Robert Shetterly

ROBERT SHETTERLY began his artistic career in Maine as an illustrator for *Farmstead* magazine. Later, he did the editorial page drawings for *Maine Times* for twelve years. He has illustrated thirty books, but he is known primarily as a painter and printmaker. His work is in collections across the U. S. and Europe. He is president of the Union of Maine Visual Artists and producer of the UMVA's Maine Masters Project, an ongoing series of video documentaries of Maine artists.

6/10   Clearcut   Robert Shetterly

THE VIEW FROM MY SPRUCE

Bernd Heinrich

In mid-May, when I last climbed this tree, I photographed a forest panorama. Far and wide the poplars and birches were then leafing out, turning a light pea green. The red maples had not yet put out leaves and their gray twigs were highlighted with burgundy blossoms. Flowering shadbush and cherry trees shone in white patches among the light greens of erupting poplar leaves and the dark black greens of evergreen firs and spruces. This year (not the previous nor next), all the sugar maples were resplendent with small lemon-yellow flowers dangling loosely at the ends of the twigs. Now, in early August, the vista all around is one of almost uniform green.

As I scan the vast expanse I see the forest from this grand view fade to a blue haze in the distance where all detail is lost. Nevertheless, a few white pines tower up like black jagged teeth on the ridge top of Kinney's Head two miles away.

The impression from my spruce, even though it is on the top of a hill, is of being in a huge green bowl. The bowl is formed by Kinney's Head, Gleason Mountain, Wilder Hill, Bald Mountain, Saddleback, Houghton Ledge, Mount Blue, Tumbledown, and Jackson. Waters that rise in these hills eventually make their way into both the Androscoggin and Kennebec Rivers. Solid unbroken forest is all around me, stretching far beyond my vision, for hundreds of miles. It is one of the few such forests remaining in the world. The forest regulates the water flow from the frequent heavy rains. It prevents floods, providing steady runoff into the trout-filled streams. It used to support salmon runs. Such a forest is also the diffuse lung tissue of the earth to which we are irrevocably bound. It is not our "environment." It is us.

Note: This passage is adapted from Bernd Heinrich, *The Trees in My Forest*, HarperCollins, Publishers, Inc., 1997, pages 20–24.

BERND HEINRICH has been a "Mainer" for fifty-three years. He grew up on Maine farms and worked in the Allagash marking trees for International Paper Co. (where they were doing selective cutting) while he studied forestry and biology at the University of Maine at Orono. In the fall, he still hunts deer near the log cabin he built in his woods near Mount Blue. Several of his books—*Bumblebee Economics, In a Patch of Fireweed, One Man's Owl, A Year in the Maine Woods, The Trees in My Forest, Ravens in Winter, The Mind of the Raven,* and *The Winter World*—are based on his research, ramblings, and ruminations near his home ground in western Maine. Before returning to Maine, he studied at the University of California at Los Angeles, was a professor of entomology at the University of California at Berkeley and a professor of biology at the University of Vermont.

Modern life, aside from providing for many of our medical and material needs, has left us hungry for spiritual and aesthetic connections to something that is elemental and far more complex and vital than anything man can create. As a painter, I find nature that is in a state of wilderness (or substantially returning to wilderness) to be disquieting and inspiring at the same time. It stirs my senses and emotions like nothing else. Knowing that I do not need to subdue the environment, I can be respectfully awed by my experience in it, take my inspiration, and leave it as I found it.

TOM HIGGINS studied at Maryville College in Tennessee and the University of Wisconsin at Madison. Collections include: the U. S. Department of State; Bates College; American Council on Education; Senator George Mitchell; Mary Herman and former Governor Angus King, Jr. His work has been featured in *Maine Art Now* and *The Art of Maine in Winter*. He is currently professor of art at the University of Maine at Farmington.

CLOUD-CAPPED

J. Thomas R. Higgins

Oil on linen, 30 x 30 inches.

DIRTY WORD

Phyllis Austin

The notion that it is impossible to have any more wilderness in Maine than we already have goes against nature and good sense.

One only has to walk into a cut-over area that has been left alone to see how insistent the land is in regenerating itself.

If humans don't interfere, seedlings will evolve over years into mature trees and eventually into old growth. That's an inexorable law of natural forces, even if we don't often give it a chance to prove itself.

But the forest industry and the "drive everywhere" motor-user lobby hate the very word wilderness, fearing it will interfere with their making money or having fun.

They are behind the effort to convince Mainers that wilderness means virgin forest completely untouched by humans.

Their "true wilderness" doesn't exist presently in Maine except in a few places already protected by law. Since there's no more, they assert, there's no reason to talk about the issue any longer.

They are misinformed, at best. They are denying the ecological reality of how a forest ages, as well as the human need to experience the natural world in its most sacred form—wilderness.

As nonsensical and scientifically flawed as it is, the anti-wilderness strategy has worked. It effectively has turned the whole subject of wilderness on its head for more than a decade, dividing people into opposing camps and providing fertile ground for mean-spiritedness, half-truths, and short-sightedness.

In the political arena, wilderness has become a dirty word. The aim of "stakeholders" representing the forest-products industry, sportsmen's organizations, and motorized recreation is to taint the word so completely that it drops out of our common usage and, by extension, out of environmental debate and negotiation.

Complicit in the undermining of wilderness are policymakers and bureaucrats. They have bent to the pressure of wilderness opponents. They have backed off from using the word wilderness in laws and regulations and blocked creation or expansion of wilderness areas on state park and public reserved lands.

Leading environmental groups have gone along to get along. The monumental changes in forestland ownership of the last dozen years have provided unparalleled opportunities for conservation protection. To be a player, environmentalists have avoided the "W" word for fear it would marginalize them as "lefties."

Now, at the beginning of a new, very challenging century, those of us who love wilderness—the word and its values—must put away our silence.

We have long been too polite, too apologetic, and too fearful. There will be no chance of establishing large wilderness landscapes in Maine's future unless we fight for them—as if this were our last chance.

It's time to say *wilderness* at every opportunity (surely it's a more poetic term than backcountry/non-motorized) and not be afraid to show our passion for it. Without the word, how do we talk about the wilderness concept of places "untrammeled" by humankind or the wilderness experience of paddling or hiking for days on end in peace and quiet.

Much of the debate over what wilderness is (in Maine and elsewhere) and what it means goes back to the definition of wilderness set out in the 1964 federal Wilderness Act.★

But many of my friends talk about wilderness, dream about it, and venture into it without knowing anything about the Act. I hear them call every patch of woods in Maine wilderness, seemingly thrilled and inspired by puckerbrush as much as they are by 200-year-old sugar maples.

While I sometimes try to correct them on what wilderness is or isn't, according to the landmark Act, I don't offer to remake their interpretation of what's beautiful. It makes me think there's something to be learned here about the inherent roominess in such spiritually evocative words.

National conservation icons Aldo Leopold and Bob Marshall, astute policymakers, lawyers, and scientists all struggled over a 40-year period to come up with a statutory definition of wilderness. Their efforts—and subsequent squabbling over the meaning of wilderness in Washington and Augusta—tell us it's no easy matter to come up with a universally acceptable definition.

When I came to Maine in 1969 as a political journalist, the term I most frequently heard to describe the state's vast timberlands was "the wildlands." That word was used interchangeably with "wilderness" or "the Maine woods."

At the time, there was no protected land with wilderness in its name except for the Allagash Wilderness Waterway, established in 1966 by state statute. The Hundred-Mile Wilderness corridor (an unofficial name given to it by *Backpacker* magazine) of the Appalachian Trail was not completely protected at that time and would not be until the mid-'90s.

Starting in 1931, Governor Percival P. Baxter began piecing together lands around Katahdin to create Baxter State Park, now 204,733 acres with 80 percent of it in the highest protective category of "sanctuary." He was adamant that the park, bought with his own personal fortune for the people of Maine, was to be "forever wild" (aside from the 28,000 acres he directed to be managed as a showplace for "exemplary" forestry).

There was local rancor over Baxter's enterprise as he expanded the preserve and banned hunting in popular areas. Over the years, Governor Baxter's gift and legend triumphed over many peoples' unease with wilderness—at least there on those particular acres. But some sportsmen's undying loathing of wilderness surfaced in the late '90s when the park expanded slightly on the West Branch of the Penobscot River and proposed banning hunting, trapping, and motorized access on that 2,269-acre parcel.

"Wild lands" (meaning undeveloped, uncultivated lands) is a term that was used in connection with grants of Maine land to various people long before Maine became a state in 1820. Stanley Bearce Attwood's 1946 compendium on civil divisions, *The Length and Breadth of Maine,* defined wild land as "a minor civil division, unincorporated and unorganized, in which property is assessed and taxes are levied directly by the state."

The effort to eliminate the word "wilderness" and to block creation of large wilderness areas in Maine can be easily traced back to the beginnings in 1971 of the Land Use Regulation Commission (LURC), the planning and zoning board for the 10.5 million acres of unorganized territory. This was land in private ownership, held mostly by the pulp and paper companies, and they fought hard against the proposed new agency.

The wild lands became well known as "the wildlands" (a regulated jurisdiction) under LURC. In fact, the first LURC bill introduced in 1967 would have established the Wildlands Use Regulation Commission.

In LURC's first Comprehensive Land Use Plan (CLUP) in 1976, the agency attempted to influence the public's view of that great forest landscape. The introduction called the jurisdiction a "relatively wild, natural area. Some argue that none of the jurisdiction meets the [federal] definition of wilderness because of land and timber management and recreational use," it said. "Depending on the level of forest management in the area, once harvested, a region is left to nature for anything from ten to eighty years. Forest flora and fauna grow and live until natural succession again produces tree growth of some economic value. Thus, although the area is not virgin forest, it is relatively inaccessible, and it does have a natural character," the plan said.

Further on, it said, "The Maine Woods is an important part of what the state stands for. Baxter State Park, the Allagash Wilderness Waterway, Acadia National Park, and the Maine Coast would lose much of their meaning and value without the backdrop of the vast woodlands to the north."

As long as the timber industry was using the rivers to drive logs to market, what the woods were called wasn't a major issue. Timber country was largely inaccessible to the public because road access was limited.

But when the last of the river drives ended by the mid-'70s, the companies began a massive expansion of their then modest road system to haul wood by truck. Recreationists and tourists poured in over industry lands, and they were horrified at the big clearcuts they saw for the first time.

Industry realized it was in their interest that the public not think of their lands as wildlands or wilderness. They coined the term "working forest" to foster the image of a domesticated landscape—a tree farm, if you will, not a place of wildness that might spark protection initiatives. Also, the landowners wanted the public to know, in case it didn't, that almost all of that great woods out there was owned privately and provided jobs that kept a lot of northern communities alive and well.

The word problem showed up pointedly in 1983 at a public hearing in Fort Kent where LURC was taking testimony on proposed changes to its comprehensive plan. An industry lobbyist said the paper companies could live with the proposed revisions but demanded that LURC replace the terms wildlands and wilderness with working forest.

LURC didn't concede. But industry didn't give up. On every occasion at meetings and forums, they pushed "working forest" as reality-on-the-ground and what was best for Maine's economy. Wilderness was slammed as something devilish and threatening.

"Working forest" was popularized among the general public in the late '80s and early '90s during the work of the Northern Forest Lands Council and in the debate over the Forest Practices Act. The word "wildlands" became almost obsolete in common usage and regulatory reference.

During that period, environmentalists bickered among themselves over how much they could afford politically to be identified as wilderness advocates, and tensions increased when the new kid on the block, RESTORE, proposed a national park and wilderness preserve of 3.2 million acres around Baxter State Park.

In the marketplace, however, wilderness was becoming increasingly salable. L. L. Bean Inc., real estate companies, tourist facilities, outfitters, sporting camps, and guides touted the word wilderness and the wilderness experience in ads for hiking boots, accommodations, and fishing trips. City folk were hungry for an escape "back to nature," and, on the East Coast, the closest to fabled wilderness was northern Maine. Some companies even advertised "wilderness weddings" as part of "the Maine experience."

Global competition and financial ups-and-downs caught up with the pulp and paper companies and other large landowners in the '90s, and millions of acres of forestland were broken up and resold to the highest bidders, such as short-term investment groups and liquidation harvesters. Suddenly, the state, land trusts, and other conservation interests found themselves staring at acquisition possibilities beyond their wildest dreams—from pockets of precious rare plants to landscape-scale forest and wildlife habitat.

But no matter how nicely and softly the word wilderness was broached, the mention of it was electrifying. Property rights advocates had organized into a powerful lobby for the Northern Forest Lands debate, and long after the council's study was done, they hammered away at wilderness. Wilderness, they claimed, meant a federal takeover of private lands and restrictions or bans on motorized access. They helped fan the fire against a national park, calling the idea anathema to good, God-loving people.

When LURC began revising its comprehensive land use plan in 1996, environmentalists, wanting to avoid battle over the "W" word, did not push for a wilderness zone but supported a "natural character" zone instead. The influence of industry was evident in the final plan adopted by LURC. In a slap at wilderness advocates, it stated that LURC wouldn't establish specific natural character zones on its own; that would be done only if and when major landowners wanted to go that way.

In fact, the plan, at the behest of one commissioner, included a wilderness disclaimer: in the definition for wildlands, the plan said "wildlands" was a term "which has commonly been used to describe the commission's jurisdiction, a term which is not synonymous with wilderness nor is it intended to imply that the area is not under active forest management."

In the strongest statement ever approved by a commission, the plan further stated: "While the more undeveloped portion of the jurisdiction is often referred to as wilderness by recreationists or those promoting recreation in the jurisdiction, this area is not wilderness by strict definition. To visitors, much of this area may seem like wilderness compared to most of the rest of the Northeast. For those living or working in or near the mainland portion of the jurisdiction, however, logging roads and active timber harvesting clearly identify the region as a managed forest important to the forest industry and segments of the recreation industry in the state."

Increasingly uncomfortable with their avoidance of the word "wilderness," environmentalists stopped playing the word game by the end of the decade—at least in some important forums. The chance to reclaim "wilderness" came at meetings to rewrite the Integrated Resource Plan (IRP), the overall management plan for the state's public lands and parks. During the two and a half years of discussion prior to adoption of the revisions by the Bureau of Parks and Lands (BPL), environmentalists on the citizen advisory committee pushed wilderness, wilderness, wilderness.

The bureau had indicated that the IRP process would be the appropriate forum for discussing the creation of a wilderness category on some public lands. But this suggestion turned out to be a baiting tactic to dissuade environmentalists from demanding a wilderness zone when individual public land plans were up for renewal.

The intensity of resistance to wilderness by the forest industry, hunters, and motorized users was palpable to anyone attending the committee meetings; and, to boot, BPL's director flatly said that no one on his staff involved in the policy process supported wilderness areas. This key debate mostly escaped the public eye due to the lack of media attention.

In the end, the bureau outlawed a wilderness category. The agency agreed, however, to take what it deemed "the essence" of wilderness values and incorporate them into zoning categories more acceptable to the bureau and the majority of the advisory panel.

The words BPL came up with as wilderness substitutes were: backcountry/non-motorized, natural areas, and ecological reserve categories. Those, the bureau promised, would encompass many of the attributes associated with wilderness. Wilderness advocates pointed out, to no avail, that wilderness by another name is not the same.

The IRP wilderness debate was a skirmish compared to the intense conflict over the Allagash Wilderness Waterway, a conflict also brought on by revision of a BPL management plan, in this case, the plan for the renowned 92-mile canoe route. This battle, however, became a real donnybrook and took on national significance because of the waterway's designation as a federal Wild and Scenic River.

Activists tried to strengthen the regulations and put forth a new vision to enhance the wilderness character of the Allagash. But again, the forest industry and motorized advocates ruled the day. They argued at every opportunity that the Allagash had been domesticated by the logging, farming, and old-fashioned outdoors activities of generations of "Moosetowners." It hadn't been a "real wilderness" for a very long time, they contended, concluding that therefore there was no reason to discuss the Allagash as a wilderness.

Meanwhile, elsewhere in state government, the disappearance of the word wilderness continued in mysterious ways. The word was inexplicably eliminated from the Land for Maine's Future statute. When this deletion was discovered, the program's director made sure the word was reinserted, hoping the deletion had been an oversight, rather than a surreptitious act.

Each new assault against wilderness provoked the question: How could such a lovely word and concept, beloved by so many people, become such a tar baby? Doug Scott of the Pew Wilderness Center has painstakingly sorted out the history of the Wilderness Act, and his findings provide important insights into why wilderness is so threatening to its opponents. Scott attributes much of the problem to confusion over the words "untrammeled" and "untrampled."

Many people use those two words interchangeably, but they are very different in meaning. "Untrammeled" means "unconfined" or "unencumbered," so an untrammeled landscape is one in which the forces of nature have free rein. Although "trample" and "tramp" usually suggest stepping heavily or crushing under-foot, they can also mean simply to walk or travel about on foot.

With eyes wide open, according to Scott, Congress accepted "untrammeled" to refer to a "condition" of land to be designated wilderness. There was no intention, he says, to create wilderness areas where humans could not visit and "tramp."

Furthermore, Scott says, Congress fully intended that wilderness designation would be granted to abused lands, recognizing that lands in the eastern U. S. in particular had a past history of heavy cutting. It was the U. S. Forest Service that later put forth a "purity" concept that distorted the intent of the Wilderness Act in order to stave off wilderness initiatives in the West. Along the way, Scott says, the Forest Service came up with substitute categories for wilderness—heritage areas, pioneer zones, and back-country—none of which were given the legal protections of wilderness.

It's incomprehensible to me that wilderness—the word and the reality—could become endangered in Maine. Wilderness is singularly evocative to the soul and is powerfully embedded in the state's history and mystique.

I often try to look into the hearts of those who would kill wilderness while enjoying "the outdoors"—people I have known for many years. The only explanation I can come up with is that they can't let themselves love nature as deeply as wilderness asks them to.

In the end, the battle over wilderness, personal and political, is about self-control and restraining destructive human activities. This is not an age that recognizes the value of limits; in fact, it encourages blatant gluttony. But only by setting limits can we preserve the full richness of the natural world that wilderness embodies.

*The 1964 Wilderness Act defines wilderness as ". . . an area where the earth and its community of life are untrammeled by man, where man himself is a visitor who does not remain. An area of wilderness is further defined to mean in this Act an area of undeveloped Federal land retaining its primeval character and influence, without permanent improvements or human habitation, which is protected and managed so as to preserve its natural conditions and which . . . generally appears to have been affected primarily by the forces of nature, with the imprint of man's work substantially unnoticeable; [and] . . . has outstanding opportunities for solitude or a primitive and unconfined type of recreation. . . ." (A source of further information is www.pew wildernesscenter.org.)

PHYLLIS AUSTIN has been a journalist for thirty-seven years, first with the *Associated Press* and then with *Maine Times,* where she wrote about environmental and other public policy issues for twenty-six years. She has received two major journalism fellowships—the Alicia Patterson Fellowship, which provided support for a year-long study of Maine's paper industry, and the John S. Knight Fellowship at Stanford University—as well as other professional study fellowships. She has been recognized for her environmental writing and journalistic achievements by the Maine legislature, the University of Southern Maine, the University of Maine at Orono, and environmental organizations. Currently, she is a freelance reporter and is working on book projects.

Red Fox in Snow
Vulpes vulpes

D. D. Tyler

Like the fox, the quality of our lives rests upon that of the natural world and we must keep an eye on it.

D. D. Tyler's bio can be found on page 20.

Gramp's Gift

Greg Shute

I was raised on the coast, on the shores of Penobscot Bay, but I never connected to the ocean the way I have with the rivers and lakes of Maine. Perhaps it was because the Penobscot Bay of my youth was not the boating paradise of today. No, the Penobscot Bay—or, more specifically, the Belfast Bay—that I knew in my early years was filled with effluent from poultry processing plants. The Bay was not a place for recreation in those days, and I was drawn inland to the clear waters of lakes and rivers.

My appreciation for wild places started early, and I have my Grandfather to thank. When I was two years old, Gramp bought land on a pond a few miles from home. Over the next couple years, he and my father cleared the site and built a cabin. Our camp is a rustic place, and from the time I was four until I went away to college, I spent every summer there. As soon as my brother and I got out of school, my family would move out for the summer. As I grew older, I was able to stay at camp by myself while my parents worked. The pond was my playground. I fished, caught turtles, snakes, and frogs and explored the nearby woods. I did not think too much about the education I was getting at the time—kids usually do not—but now as I look back I see the influence this place had on me and how it shaped who I have become and the choices I have made in life.

Gramp was nearing the end of his life when he bought the property. I am sure that it was a stretch for him to purchase the land. However, I am convinced that he saw the camp and the experiences that our family would have there as his legacy to future generations. Our camp is not in a remote area of the North Woods. It is located on a pond in Waldo County just a couple miles inland from busy Route One. Over the past forty years a handful of new camps have been built, but the view from our place is that which my grandfather experienced when he bought the land and the same that I saw first as a two-year-old. The shoreline that we look at stretches, undeveloped, for over a mile to Ducktrap Mountain. Recently I sat on the porch as the last rays of a weak November sun illuminated the pines on the far shore. I was reminded how thankful I am that my son can experience this place just as I did as a child. Except for the natural succession that will take place over time, the shoreline within our view will remain unchanged forever thanks to the vision of a nearby property owner and local land trust.

Like most Maine kids, I grew up at a time when a small patch of woods was within easy walking or biking distance from home. My friends and I spent all our free time there, building forts, fishing, trapping, and tramping about. As I grew older, my explorations took me farther afield. First to a larger patch of woods in town and then to the Camden Hills, Baxter State Park, the Allagash and St. John, and the Canadian wilds.

After high school, college was chosen for its Outdoor Education program and proximity to the North Woods of Maine. Upon graduation, I was fortunate to find work in the outdoor field. Today I manage a wilderness program for a non-profit organization. I am fortunate that my duties allow me to spend a healthy amount of time in the field guiding canoe trips. Over the years, I have had the opportunity to travel through much of Maine's backcountry. I have spent entire summers leading teenagers on extended canoe trips. I paddled for five summers in the Mistassini Reserve of Quebec with native Cree guides. I regularly take groups to canoe the rivers of Northern Quebec and Labrador and more recently, Baffin Island in the Arctic. I have experienced what most would consider wilderness. I have shared campfires with friends hundreds of miles from the nearest road as wolves howled just beyond the firelight. I have been humbled as my canoe was surrounded by thousands of caribou as they swam across Quebec's George River on their annual migration. In addition, I have experienced a primal fear while on a trip on the Soper River of Baffin Island. I looked down to see my foot beside a fresh polar bear track, and I quickly realized that this was a place where man was not the top predator.

Recently I took a solo canoe trip on the St. John River after a party canceled at the last minute. I had my heart set on what has turned into my annual pilgrimage from Baker Lake to Allagash village, so I headed north. I wanted to see spring arrive in the North Woods. I slipped my canoe into Baker Lake and quickly headed downstream. I didn't see anyone for the first two days and was giddy with the excitement of rising when I wanted and stopping at sites that I had always hoped to explore. I watched the courtship flight of woodcock and discovered bloodroot and Dutchman's breeches blooming. As the swift current carried me along, I had plenty of time to daydream, and I could not help but think what an incredible river the St. John is. I recalled what George Elson, the Cree guide for Mina Hubbard's 1905 trip across Labrador, said when referring to Quebec's George River. After a long day's paddle George was looking out over the river and was asked what he was thinking and he replied, "I was thinking how proud I am of this river." I feel the same pride for the St. John. Thanks to The Nature Conservancy, much of the land surrounding the St. John has been preserved in recent years, forever ensuring this beautiful river will be available to future wilderness paddlers.

Near the end of my trip the weather warmed, and I found the first fiddleheads of the season on a sandy south-facing riverbank. I harvested just enough for my supper, being careful not to take too many from one spot. Later I fished at the mouth of Chimenticook Stream. I cast a Mickey Finn into the swirling water and soon had a respectable brook trout on the shore. I do not keep many of the fish I catch these days, but the trout I caught was quickly killed and put on the last of my ice in the cooler. The evenings feast of brook trout and fiddleheads connected me to the river in a way that I can never fully articulate.

There is growing momentum in Maine to preserve our wild areas. I recently had the opportunity to paddle in the Debsconeag Lakes region, a short raven's flight west of Katahdin. The Nature Conservancy's recent purchase of this land will ensure that the area remains a wilderness of small lakes and ponds where people can paddle past ancient trees and undeveloped shoreline, explore ice caves, and carry their canoes over ancient portage trails. Areas like the Debsconeags need to be set aside. As Sigurd Olsen writes, "If we can somehow retain places where we can always sense the mystery of the unknown, our lives will be richer."

A night beside the West Branch of the Penobscot River a couple years ago caused me to be hopeful for the future of Maine's North Woods. Our group was camped at Pine Stream just before the West Branch empties into Chesuncook. The summer's lack of rain and the low water of Chesuncook exposed Pine Stream Falls for the first time in seventy-five years. Earlier in the day, we explored a muddy riverbank that in a normal year is covered by the lake's water. We saw the tracks of moose, coyote, fox, deer, and bear.

As dusk settled we gathered for a group howl in hopes that any nearby coyotes might serenade us. Our howl was quickly answered, and we listened to the yips and yaps of a group of coyotes off to the east, the same familiar choruses that I hear regularly at home coming from the Sheepscot River valley just outside my bedroom window. The coyotes stopped as quickly as they started, and there was silence again. We sat in the quiet around the spruce fire, and a lone deep howl filled the star-studded night. It came from a point we had explored earlier in the day, a short paddle from our campsite. I have seen and heard a number of wolves while paddling through the Canadian wilds. I'm not convinced that it wasn't a wolf that we heard that evening, but for all of us sitting around the campfire it really didn't matter. For a few short moments we experienced the mystery of the Maine Woods as the howl touched a primitive spot buried deep inside us all.

I am hopeful that our legacy is a Maine that is wild enough to support a resident pack of wolves and to provide what former Supreme Court Justice and wilderness advocate William O. Douglas referred to as an "element of mystery and awe."

GREG SHUTE, a Maine native and Maine Guide, is the Wilderness Programs Director at the Chewonki Foundation in Wiscasset, where he has worked since 1984. He lives near the Sheepscot River in Alna with his wife Lynne and son Kyle.

BILL CURTSINGER is a professional photographer and photojournalist, with thirty-three published articles in *National Geographic* magazine; his work has also appeared in every major magazine worldwide. Based in Yarmouth, Curtsinger writes the text for many of his stories and has co-authored five books with his photographs. His photographic themes include underwater, nature, science, archaeology, indigenous cultures, environmental issues, and various photojournalism subjects. He has produced video shorts and clips, as well as a library of stock video footage. Curtsinger is also a founding member of the Maine-based art group "10 x10." www.billcurtsingerphoto.com

St. John River

Bill Curtsinger

Thoreau in the Maine Woods

Morning
I rose early, never content
as were my tent mates, to let the watery dream
be more or less than it was. So I went again
to the stream where they had really fished for trout
or I dreamed they had and again the ravenous
darting multitude rose sparkling to test
the truth of dreams. Squirming Chivin, silvery Roach,
and speckled Trout made impossible rainbow arcs
in the moonlight against the sleeping mass
of Mt. Ktaadn. At last the companions woke.
The waters made flesh fed and refreshed them.

Afternoon
Moose-men. Wood-eaters. Had I not found you
I must have made you. Perfect forest denizens.
Stick-legged rough barked moss humped
antlers grown as lichen on the rock.
We almost passed you as you stood frozen
on the edge of flight. The birch canoe
backpedaling, the hunter, as best he could,
fired over our heads. Suddenly it was
as if you'd never been. But I knew now
your necessity. A found reality to fit
a space, a void made evident by vanishing.
When Joe Polis with his pocketknife skinned out
the one that dropped a hundred yards away
milk swirled with blood in shallow water.

Night
Deep in the forest with Indian Joe.
Wildness, I say, is the preservation
of mankind. (Perverse Hamlet declaiming
to Not Be is To Be). A distant tree falls.
Not from any animal or human agency—

just falls, ultimately. The soft sound
reaches us. The camp fire burns on without
ominous flicker or flare. Where
mankind is finally preserved from harm, there
trees fall safely with soft sounds.

The Second Morning
Behind us as in a dream
the raw, red carcass lies
half in, half out of the stream.
We paddle first with firmness, then
with desperation. Glancing back,
the bend we thought to round
and thus protect us is straight now
as the main street of Concord. Walls,
steeples of trees lean in on either hand.
The stream as in a dream contracts, sweeping
us back exhausted on the twisted pillow.

—Robert M. Chute

(Thoreau's evocation of wildness is from the introduction of his essay, "Walking." His dying words are reported to have been "Moose—Indians.")

ROBERT M. CHUTE is the author of poems in eight chapbooks and a wide variety of journals. He won the Walsh Poetry Prize from *Beloit Poetry Journal* and a Maine state chapbook award. A native of Naples, his father was an innkeeper and his mother a school teacher. Chute was educated at the University of Maine at Orono and Johns Hopkins University. Chute is professor emeritus of biology at Bates College and has done research in parasitology and limnology. He has been writing since age fourteen.

NEVER LET GO THE DREAM

Garrett Conover

Given a magic wand to create wildness in the remnants of the Maine Woods, I would consider the following as starting assumptions:

• Acknowledge that the essence of the deep woods is river based. Rivers were the travel routes winter and summer before road proliferation. Despite the prevalence of ponds and lakes, the travel routes are largely riverine.

• Acknowledge that quiet users and motor users are completely incompatible groups and that habitat for each must be established and maintained.

• Any preserve must be big and nearly roadless. "Wilderness" should be the goal, despite the fact that multiple generations and hundreds of years will need to pass before restoration can come close to such an ideal. Any lesser goal will lead to failure at worst, mediocrity at best. Many people may not think such a high goal important, but aiming high will get us farther than we can expect to get from aiming at a much easier target.

I would prefer a federal wilderness designation. This would yield all the advantages of federal protection without the superstructure, overhead, and concessions associated with national park status. However, either wilderness or national park designation are preferable to state management, which is inevitably volatile, subject to changing political pressures, and very subject to special interests, especially if those interests are wealthy global corporations eager to capitalize on a relatively poor state's permanent or periodic desperation.

Both state and federal management agencies of wild areas may have admirable missions, goals, and attributes. But both also suffer from inefficiencies, political and bureaucratic pressures, and inertia. The bigger, more unwieldy federal agencies will do less immediate good or harm and be slower in doing it. Their cumbersomeness has the positive aspect of providing some useful stability that allows different constituencies more time to work out compromises and then do what is best for the greatest number of people.

State management is much more volatile because of the rapid turnover of administrations and the resulting changes in goals and in attention given to wild regions. Change can come faster and be harder to reverse. This is exactly what makes a place like Maine so attractive to multinationals in extractive industries. They know they can buy what they need at a price that is cost-effective to pay. Steamrolling through state hurdles is infinitely easier and cheaper than steamrolling through the hurdles of a federal bureaucracy.

If the above generalities are true, or at least true enough, what wildlands vision might emerge?

Personally, I would like to see a large core area protected with special attention given to the watersheds that contain the best of the remaining canoe country. The premier canoe routes, such as the St. John, Allagash, the Upper West Branch of the Penobscot, and the Caucomgomoc and Loon Lake area, should have special protection and be motor free. All but the major roads should not only be abandoned but also decommissioned in a manner that encourages their return to impassable forest as quickly as possible. In place of the current token beauty strips, the watersheds should be protected by significant forest regeneration extending back from the water's edge for at least one-half mile but preferably more.

Outside the classic and best canoe areas, such a preserve could be managed less intensively, and motor use would be part of the picture. Some lakes within the canoe areas would probably retain some grandfathered motor provision for residents of places like Chesuncook Village and of some long-standing sporting camps.

In developing such a preserve, we can learn from other areas. Many policies instituted in the 1.2 million-acre Boundary Waters

Canoe Area Wilderness (BWCAW) in northern Minnesota would also be applicable in Maine. In the BWCAW, even the Forest Service rangers do not use motors but canoe, ski, snowshoe, and dog-sled like everyone else. Small aircraft are not allowed within 3,000 feet of the lake surfaces. Only in case of emergency or of other extraordinary conditions are motors used inside the Wilderness boundary.

The area is buffered by the Superior National Forest, where all other uses including motorized ones are allowed. Similarly, in Voyageurs National Park, where power boats and snowmobile use make the area unappealing to quiet users, the needs of those interested in motor recreation are also met.

Because the region offers both a world-class wilderness area and multiple-use options, all segments of the outdoor industry are accommodated. In 1985 quiet users alone pumped $28 million into the small end-of-the-road town of Ely, population six thousand, one of the primary jumping-off points for the BWCAW.

At present, here in Maine, the motor-user lobby holds all the power and all the cards and has the ear of the politicians. Maine is not able to deliver anything to the wilderness-oriented canoeist or winter traveler on even the best of the remaining routes. To reap the benefits of this segment of the tourism industry, an area must deliver the goods. Maine at present cannot and does not. People go elsewhere, and a significant segment of the tourism dollar is consequently lost.

Quiet users who do continue to come do so not because of a high-quality experience but because Maine is convenient to reach and has the illusion of being wilder than other areas in northern New England. Banking on an area being relatively wilder is the most certain path toward irreversible degradation.

If a premier experience were available, the tourism economy would be diversified; visitors would come and gladly put up with regulations and management requirements that preserve the integrity of an area. But the experience must deliver, and a region that defaults to the motor interests only precludes diversity, quality, and economic potential. An area that can deliver to both quiet users and motor users gains everything, reduces conflict, and adds significantly to regional and local economies without losing the hefty input from the spin-off economies supported by all recreationists.

Quiet users are no more a bunch of elitist, over-educated, left-leaning, libertarian, granola-crunching, home-schooling, organic-farming pantheists driving fancy foreign cars and funded by money made elsewhere than motor users are fat, local, narrow-minded xenophobic rednecks with tunnel vision, lack of imagination, paranoid views, and a congenital fear of anything from away. However, there are enough people in each camp who actually do fit these descriptions and so perpetuate the caricatures. The resulting standoff makes building trust and understanding almost impossible and consequently prevents the conversations that could reveal common goals and produce strategies to attain them. Wouldn't it be nice to get such conversations going? It just might lead to balance and a division of resources that would provide for most of the needs of most of the interested parties.

But in case these conversations don't take place anytime soon, we better continue to purchase development rights and help The Nature Conservancy and every other environmental organization that is taking steps in the right direction. We should even applaud the Kingdom Purchasers for protecting some areas even if we as the public don't get to go into them. Maybe in the end, enough people will recognize the wisdom of designating a large preserve, and then we will all benefit by being able to go to the appropriate areas for the kind of experience we want. I would happily portage, paddle, pole, or snowshoe beyond the reach of the motor users. And I bet they would be happy to be free in their own regions.

The gas merchants, the motel and B & B owners, the restaurateurs, and the equipment dealers, and many others would be happy to welcome all users. Our fighting and bickering would be reduced because we'd each have access to our favored habitat. Best of all, if the preserved places were big enough, delivered on most counts, and were maybe even downright inspiring, we'd all be back, again and again.

And because a large-scale federal preserve functions democratically, all of us are invited, limited only by our willingness to go there quietly if some sections require it or to share it with motorized recreationists where that is appropriate. Since recreation is not extractive, the resource remains as a sustainable product that, in the face of escalating population pressures, becomes ever more valuable. Of course that option takes vision, commitment, resources, planning, and endless vigilance and negotiation—in short, a life sentence of very difficult work.

Or we can deliberately scuttle everything by simply doing nothing, defaulting to the loudest, most demanding faction, which at the moment is the motor lobby that wants access to every lake, pond, and puddle in the state. Without organized opposition willing to pay for wilderness, they'll get what they want. Not only is the noise of their motors loud in the woods, their voices are loud and organized in Augusta, and their trail of easy spin-off dollars is significant.

The odd thing is that the motor recreationists regard the quiet users as elitist. For the cost of their trucks, trailers, boats, motors, ATVs, snowmobiles, lodging, gas, maintenance, and overhead, quiet users can disappear into the Canadian wilds for weeks or months at a time and for years on end. And they will. As long as Maine refuses to deliver anything to the quiet users, they are going to go elsewhere. Anyone who doubts this should read the brochures of the most renowned Maine Guide services catering to quiet users. Certainly there are Maine trips, but virtually all lead trips to the Canadian North, and some reach even farther afield to Greenland, Baffin Island, Siberia, and Scandinavia.

With a serious wilderness preserve that could meet quiet users' needs, that picture would change. Collectively, quiet users are an economic force smaller than the motor lobby but vital and well worth courting in times of an uncertain economy and of rising gas prices. Some diversity is always better than no diversity, and every gateway community next to a premier wilderness area does better when it acknowledges this. With some discipline and forethought, no community need fall into the trap of allowing glitzy, two-bit development to line its roads, either. There are plenty of examples of what no control leads to in those places that experienced explosive growth at a time when zoning was not seen as sensible and productive. Why should it be so difficult to emulate the good examples and shun the bad? Perhaps because it takes work, communication, compromise, and rigorous planning—all difficult tasks when participants' dreams are different and in some cases, in conflict. Default doesn't take much work or care. It just happens.

Visionaries are dreamers and workers and will reap some reward. Defaulters, in their laziness, are guaranteed only one thing—being pushed and shoved around by the forces they fail to control. Not a lot of happiness in that scenario. Not even a dream to let slide away, never to be recovered or restored.

In the meantime, I counteract my personal pessimism by working in any way I can for the organizations bent on saving and salvaging what is left of our own backyards, the Maine Woods, and the bigger dreams of a large, seriously managed preserve. And I'm grateful that there is something worth saving and restoring. I'm grateful, too, that it is wilder than the rest of domesticated New England. That's why I choose to stay and to fight against all odds. It is why I dare to dream and hope that this forest landscape will recover and grow wilder than it was when I first encountered it.

People like Margaret Murie, Rachel Carson, Sigurd Olson, and Aldo Leopold passed the torch down to my generation. The flame of that torch is fueled by their faith and care. I hope those of us who bear that torch now can make it burn all the brighter and encourage those who will receive it from us. I hope they will be able to draw strength from work we have done well. And may we live long enough to see and take pride in the work of those younger men and women who are not afraid to dream big.

ALEXANDRA AND GARRETT CONOVER have led canoe trips for the past twenty-three years in the open-water seasons and also snowshoe and toboggan trips to the wildest remaining areas of Maine, Quebec, and Labrador. Their guide service, North Woods Ways, has become synonymous with quality, traditional resonance, and skillful engagement with the wilds. When not on the trail with guests, the Conovers are frequently in the Quebec and Labrador bush on their own more ambitious trips or learning from Naskapi and Montagnai friends who still spend significant time on the land. Garrett is the author of *Beyond the Paddle* and co-author with Alexandra of the *Winter Wilderness Companion*.

THE DANCE

Bunny McBride

Humans were formed in delicate interaction with the animate earth. When Europeans first landed on the shores of Maine almost five centuries ago they encountered people whose lives still evidenced that fundamental relationship.

I can't contemplate Maine's remnant wilderness without thinking about its indigenous peoples, those who inhabited the place when it was whole. Fitting themselves to nature's seasonal rhythms, they celebrated times of plenty and accepted times of want. It was an intricate, often difficult dance in which humans were intimately and inextricably intertwined with all other life. It was remarkable in that these early residents aimed to avoid stepping on the toes of other beings, and if they did misstep, apologies and amends were made to ensure that all life forms remained in the dance.

In the wake of the European invasion, ruthless exploitation of natural resources wreaked biological and cultural havoc on the region's first peoples. So it is that today most of us who inhabit or visit Maine, regardless of our ethnic heritage, have forgotten how to dance with anyone but ourselves and our technologies. Moving in ever greater isolation, we humans rarely feel nature's fingers pressing the small of our backs, guiding us this way or that. Who among us can call the stars by name, let alone turn to them for direction? Who can follow a subtle scent or any other call of the wild?

Shut off from the orienting sights, sounds, rhythms, and smells of the wilderness, we run the risk of tripping over our self-centeredness—and breaking up the multiform dance that has sustained our species since time out of mind.

How exactly did that dance go? We can see it, just over history's horizon—

The first peoples in the vast sweep of land we now call Maine lived and moved among the shadows of towering pine and birch. They camped all along the banks of the region's great rivers, which flowed down from the mountains of Maine's heartland into the ocean. Never far from the Northern Atlantic seaboard, they were called Wabanaki (People of the Dawnland) by their inland neighbors, for each morning the first sunlight on the continent belonged to them. And they belonged to it, for they believed that Kisuhs, the great Sky Fire, was the ultimate spirit-power in a world in which everything was imbued with a sacred force.

During the summer, daylight came early, stayed late, and transformed the rugged region into a land of plenty. The season's bounty enabled individual families that had spent the miserly winter months inland to come together in large coastal encampments of a hundred or more people without fear of exhausting resources. There were many coastal camping sites, such as the wooded peninsula embraced by the Penobscot and Bagaduce Rivers. From the shore, the land rose gradually to a ridge overlooking the vast mouth of the Penobscot with its scattering of offshore islands to the southwest. The Bagaduce, a more modest stream, curved around the peninsula's southeast flank to join the great river as it poured into the ocean. Beyond the Bagaduce rolled spruce-covered hills, backed by the heroic silhouette of bare granite peaks on Pemeteq (Mt. Desert Island). Some days mist rolled in from the sea, blotting out landmarks and weighting the air with a damp salty scent. Other days the sky held a blueness so clear that it looked as if it might shatter—and so it did when shifting winds grabbed fistfuls of water and threw them against that crystalline sky.

While camped on the coast, men fished, hunted seals, and searched the forests for giant white birch trees whose bark they used to make canoes that were light and swift. Women wove baskets and fashioned birchbark containers; and with their children they gathered fruits, roots, nuts, and shellfish, and prepared smoked fish and dried berries to be stored with nuts for the stark winter months. While working, they chewed spruce gum, which was used to caulk canoe seams—and which kept their teeth white and strong. Throughout the warm season, everyone spent much time together, celebrating the bond of their extended families and renewing friendships with people from allied kin groups, each named for an animal such as the bear, beaver, whale, or eel.

Moving about seasonally to meet their basic needs, Wabanakis learned to respond to nature's shifting moods. Each autumn, when frost paled the meadows and fallen leaves formed bright skirts around the trees, just about everyone left the coast. Paddling and portaging inland, they scattered in small family groups for the fall hunt. Men stalked prey and tended traplines. Women skinned the animals and worked furs and hides into clothes, moccasins, and blankets to shield their families from winter's icy breath. Winter was so stingy that Wabanakis called January the "Moon that Provides Little Food Grudgingly." Even children realized that during this season everyone had to rely on their own mettle rather than on nature's meager offerings. Temperatures plunged far below freezing, and game diminished due to hibernation and migration. Hunters, wearing snowshoes and working with small dogs, managed to chase down deer and moose, cornering them in snowdrifts for the kill, and hauling the quarry home on toboggans. Other sustenance came from bark-lined root cellars stocked with provisions taken up in kinder seasons.

Throughout winter's reign Wabanaki life centered on the hearth in each family's birchbark wigwam. Glowing embers filled the air with quivering light and heightened the sweet scent of the hemlock boughs that carpeted the ground. Sitting upon fur blankets, a mother might nurse her youngest child while showing her older daughters how to mend clothes and embroider them with dyed porcupine quills. A father, crouched on his heels by the fire, would roast chunks of meat or repair his weapons. After nightfall, as children nodded off and parents and grandparents puffed their pipes, the age-old murmur of singing or storytelling danced about the shelter, mingled with smoke from the fire and pipes, and drifted out into the frigid darkness through an opening in the peak of the wigwam. Even the most difficult season had its pleasures.

Well into March, frozen waterways and deep snow hampered long-distance travel. Most Wabanakis remained inland until they received clear signs of winter's end. Before anyone explained those signs to children, they knew them—*felt* them. First came the long low groans of rivers and lakes as their frozen backs began to shrink and shift in the warming air. Then, loud as thunderclaps and swift as lightning, fractures bolted across each sheet of ice until it began to split into great slabs. Soon ice cakes floated atop open waters and out to sea. Their departure signaled spring and the arrival of "Spear-Fish Moon," when families canoed to falls and rapids to spear and net salmon, smelt, and other spawning fish. As leaves unfurled and painted the spaces between branches green, Wabanakis rode the current downriver, camping en route, gathering bird eggs and fiddlehead ferns. Then, once again, they arrived at the coast for the summer. There they stayed until the Moon of Ripening Berries waned to a mere sliver of light in the night sky.

And so went the dance, moon upon moon, generation upon generation—until strangers from across the Atlantic sailed to Wabanaki Country. Convinced of the idea that progress is primarily technological and material advancement, the newcomers never paused to learn the local dance. Cutting in, they grabbed the lead. Bent on controlling nature and its original inhabitants, they crushed them.

Between 1600 and 1900, the number of tribespeople living in Maine dropped from about 30,000 to under 1,000—and their land holdings fell from millions of acres to a few thousand. There was barely room to dance. Yet, remarkably, a handful still remembered how. One of the most notable among them was Mary Alice Nelson, born in 1903 on Indian Island, the Penobscot Reservation in Old Town. Everyone on the island called her Molly, but off the reservation she was Princess Spotted Elk, a celebrated dancer. She was a woman of roots and branches—tied to Penobscot tradition but reaching out to a wider world. Growing up on the island, she sought out elders who could tell her Penobscot legends, often exchanging chores for stories. With an enthusiasm that eclipsed that of other youngsters, she joined in ancient dances at ceremonial events in the tribal hall. From her mother she learned how to turn the year rings of brown ash trees into baskets. And through her father she discovered the rhythms and solace of nature harbored in the island's streams and remnant patches of forest. By age ten she could address the stars by name and catch a fish by hand.

Talent, beauty, and determination took Molly well beyond the bounds of Indian Island. She performed on stage and screen from New York to Hollywood to Paris. Finding European audiences more appreciative than Americans of the authentic tribal dances she wanted to perform, she lived in France for several years during the 1930s. There she fell in love with French journalist Jean Archambaud, who shared her passion for traditional artistry and rigorous hikes through natural landscapes. In 1934 they had a child together. Four years later, they married, only to be forced apart by World War II. Jean went into hiding, and Molly fled the country on foot with their little girl over the Pyrenees Mountains. Ultimately, mother and daughter made it safely back to the reservation in Maine, but Jean died in a refugee camp.

Although devastated by personal loss, Molly lived to see and contribute to the dawn of Wabanaki cultural renewal in the modern era. Beyond keeping tribal dances alive, she wrote down the Penobscot legends that she gathered as a child—age-old stories about how everything in nature came to be. She also kept diaries, rich with details about her lifelong struggle to resist assimilation while expanding her horizons.

By 1970 Molly had resettled permanently on Indian Island. One day, in the full green of spring, she sat in a chair under the apple tree in her yard. The tree grew near the house, which stood on a knoll. Looking down the slope to her left Molly could see the river and to her right the tribal graveyard. It had been an interesting week for a gray-haired woman who expected that one day soon she would lie in that cemetery. Two young Penobscot women had come by to ask her about the old days. They wanted information about the past, they said, because they needed it to build a better future. They spoke of Red Power and of getting back land stolen from Penobscots years ago. They had plans, ambitions. Molly began to tell them about the days long before a bridge had been built to link the island to the mainland. She spoke about her foremothers, about the Penobscot legends she had gathered as a child, and about snake dances in the old tribal hall. They did not stay long, but when they left, they said they would return.

And now, thinking of them, Molly had come outside with her 1925 diary, written when she was about their age. Sitting there under the pale pink blossoms in the late afternoon, she started to open her diary, only to be distracted by the trill of a woodcock somewhere near the river. Looking up, she spotted the bird in flight—his plump russet body, round gray head, long bill, and ridiculous little tail—spiraling higher and higher into the lavender sky until he passed out of sight. Moments later, he reappeared, tumbling wildly toward the earth as if he had been shot. But seconds before hitting the ground, his wings suddenly flared open, and the fellow righted himself and landed squarely on his feet in a glade alongside the river. With barely a pause, he took wing again and repeated his entire aerial mating dance. When he finished his performance, Molly called out spontaneously, "I, too, danced for life!" After watching him a bit longer, she returned to her diary. Opening the book, she read a passage written when she was twenty-two: "The fire of ambition must be first," it said. She laughed at her younger self. Not ambition, she thought, but love—of family, tradition, and the dance of life.

Since Molly's death in 1977, the Penobscots and Maine's three other tribal groups (Maliseet, Mi'kmaq and Passamaquoddy) have experienced a reversal of fortune. Their numbers have grown—and are now six times that of a century ago. They demanded and won various Native rights and federal funds to buy back some of their traditional land. Reunited with part of their aboriginal territory, they have found a big part of themselves and are in the throes of a great cultural reclamation effort.

It seems clear that culture, like the natural environment that helped to create it, is capable of regeneration. And we all make choices about what elements of the past should be kept alive and carried into the future. Will we continue the dance?

Note: Parts of this essay are adapted from the author's 1999 book, *Women of the Dawn*.

BUNNY MCBRIDE is a writer with an M.A. in anthropology. Much of her work focuses on cultural survival and wildlife conservation themes. She is author of *Women of the Dawn, Molly Spotted Elk: A Penobscot in Paris,* and *Our Lives in Our Hands: Micmac Indian Basketmakers,* and co-author of *The Audubon Society Field Guide to African Wildlife.* From 1981 to 1991, she and her husband, Dutch anthropologist Harald Prins, did historical research and community development work for the Aroostook band of Micmacs as part of the band's successful effort to gain federal recognition and funds to buy back aboriginal land. In 1999 she received a special commendation from the Maine legislature for her research and writing on the history of Native women in the state.

To really appreciate wilderness, one first has to experience a truly wild place. Baxter State Park remains one of the wildest places left in Maine today. No, not all of it; many people go to those woods these days. But most folks who go there do so just to climb the main trails of Katahdin or visit a few of the ponds near its base.

Those who seek true wilderness should hike the trails less traveled. They will soon discover the magic of a place that is still as wild as Percival Baxter, the visionary man who gave it all to the people of Maine, could have hoped for. *"Some day—maybe in your day—there won't be any really wild areas left. This park may be the only place where future generations can see Maine as it really was."*

BILL SILLIKER, JR., "The Mooseman," has photographed at many wild places in North America, with the results published in *Audubon, Backpacker, Field & Stream, National Wildlife, Outdoor Photographer, Outdoor Life and others* and in his calendars and his books—*Saving Maine; Uses for Mooses; Moose Watchers Handbook; Moose: Giants of the Northern Forest; Just Eagles; Just Loons;* and *Maine Moose Watcher's Guide.* Silliker has instructed natural photography for L. L. Bean since 1992 and is a frequent Fijufilm Professional Talent Team speaker. His web site www.camera hunter.com offers tips for photographers, and www.wild maine.com features prints of his work.

LOOKING SOUTH FROM HAMLIN RIDGE ON KATAHDIN

Bill Silliker, Jr.

THE TRAIL NORTH

Bob Cummings

The trail bisects the bony backbone of the Appalachian Mountains, eroded remains of peaks that once stood higher than Everest. Beginning on a wooded mountain in Georgia, it heads north, through spring, summer, and fall, to Katahdin's barren and often icy summit.

The trail explores wild valleys, high mountains, and great carpets of wildflowers. It traverses 300 miles of the largest unbroken forest east of the Mississippi—the northern forest that stretches from central Maine west through northern New Hampshire, Vermont, and much of New York.

Those who walk the entire 2,160 miles of this Appalachian Trail love Maine and its illusion of wildness. But it's a fragile illusion, a fragile trail through a fragile and sometimes degraded forest. The trail divides a narrow corridor, pressed in on all sides by threats of development from land investors and land speculators.

Maine once boasted of having the largest commercial forest in the East, some 15 million acres that grew the raw material needed to supply jobs for many thousands of mill workers. But times and priorities change. Two decades of overcutting have left a patchwork of clearcuts and depleted lands that increasingly no longer figure in the future plans of the giant companies that own the mills. Huge blocks of the forest—and many of the mills— have either been sold in recent years, often multiple times, or are on the market.

Few hikers notice. By world standards, Maine is a rain forest. Even degraded forests green quickly here, and eventually recover. Within a decade even sophisticated satellite imagery has difficulty distinguishing a clearcut. Only hikers sophisticated in forestry matters recognize the changing patterns and shades of green they see in the distance as stemming from decades of over-harvesting. Most see only forest as far as the eye can see, and mountains beyond mountains, stretching north and west to Quebec. For the hiker basking in the illusion of wilderness, it matters not that the forest cover is now dominated by sun-loving raspberry bushes and low value pin cherry, poplar, and red maples, not the spruce and fir that sustained Maine mills for a century.

But paradoxically, the degraded forest is more valuable than ever as the mills close, eliminate employees, and cut production. Maine forests have always been bought and sold—but in the past mostly between the giant companies that needed the trees for their mills. Sales then mostly redistributed the available trees among the various mill ownerships more efficiently. That has changed. Some of the major purchasers in recent years have been investment partnerships and insurance companies seeking wise investments for the vast pension funds they manage. As the funds need cash, these companies are cashing in on their profits. The sales are often to those who have little or no interest in providing Maine mills with logs and pulp wood.

Rather than pushing their land wares in industrial and trade publications, real estate ads for Maine's forests now target Maine "wanna be's" in such publications as *Down East* and the *New York Times*. The market now is for control of vast acreages enclosing wild lakes, mountains, and crystal-clear streams, not board feet of lumber or cords of pulp. The agents of choice are affiliates of the great New York auction houses, who find profits from selling Maine land rival those from selling multi-million-dollar paintings and antique collections. A sustainable forest, sustainable jobs, and a sustainable trail no longer figure in the equation.

Ironically, the trail through Maine, at least superficially, is wilder than ever—some think too wild. Earl Shaffer, the first person to walk the trail from end to end in one spring and summer in 1948, complained that his walk was too difficult when he returned for a fiftieth-anniversary stroll in 1998.

Three and a half decades after Congress decreed the Appalachian Trail was too valuable to be left to the vagaries of private ownership and should be publicly owned, the trail now passes almost exclusively along ridge lines and through the woods and mountains. The roads Shaffer followed in 1948 have been mostly bypassed.

Those who walk the trail north continue to see great beds of trilliums, mountain bluets, wild iris, mayflowers, startling blaze-orange azaleas, white flowering dogwood, yellow and pink lady slippers; and they revel in the joy of it all. Hikers are entranced with the national parks and forests, hill farms and woodlots, and main streets of quiet mountain towns.

Few recognize the fragile nature of the trail. Rather, hikers revel in the brisk cold days of early spring, tales of March snows, chilly April rains, the heat of summer, and the beauty of the northern forest autumn. They revel in walks above clouds, through clouds—and, occasionally, into cloudbursts.

Long-distance hikers live forever after with a trail of memories.

A giant black snake, imitating a rattler, rustles dry oak leaves as hikers ease by. Bear cubs scurry up twin saplings; an old sow disappears in the brush—scuffling, circling, protecting her young.

Long-distance hikers remember the drumming of partridge seeking mates; cries of pileated woodpeckers, red crests flashing through decaying forest; faint gobbles of wild turkeys on spring morns; turkey vultures, floating silently, seeking dinner; a bald eagle sitting motionless on the stub of a broken tree above a wild lake in the 100-mile wilderness; a tiny gray bird exploding from a trailside nest that's filled with the mouths of her hungry babies.

Hikers remember a half inch of ice in a cooking pot one Georgia morning; sixty-year-old cars rusting in an abandoned Carolina pasture; coyotes yodeling at a remote Pennsylvania shelter; Maine moose munching pond plants.

They have memories of community—a million hikers on summer walks; some three thousand through-hikers. Each year two hundred, maybe three, reach Katahdin. Laborers, philosophers, businessmen, and clergy; college grads and high-school dropouts, writers, teachers, bosses, workers—sharing blisters, adventures, sore toes, sprained knees, wild wonders.

The trail is two twenty-year-olds, jogging to catch Solo Sal to return forgotten tent poles; an eighty-year-old Tennessee grocer offering, "a ride to the top of the hill."

Some walk alone; others with friends, lovers, strangers. All share common joys, common experiences, common adventures; join in successes and tribulations; and lament mishaps, illnesses that slow, delay, or end journeys; share rain and sunshine, the woods, rocks, and hills.

But outside the national parks and forests, the trail is but a narrow corridor through the crowded eastern megalopolis. In no place is the trail corridor more fragile than in Maine. Through Maine's northern forest, great sections of the trail wind through a corridor that is only 200 feet wide. "I can reach out and touch the clear-cuts," one volunteer trail maintainer complains.

But the era of clear-cuts is ending. Now the threat is encroaching development. Typical is the 32,181-acre tract just east of Gulf Hagas with Whitecap Mountain on the north and bordered on the south by the West Branch of the Pleasant River. LandVest, which bills itself as an "Exclusive Affiliate of Christie's Great Estates," calls the area "a pristine wilderness" and a "superb forest investment." In the weeks before the first advertisement appeared in *Down East*, however, bulldozers crushed the piles of brush from past logging operations and trucks sprayed straw over the remains—creating a pretty picture of the wild mountains that surround the site, but not exactly the kind of thing needed to entice a logging contractor.

A few miles to the south, near Rangeley, Sotheby's is seeking to sell 8,000 acres of "unspoiled lakes . . . immense vistas (and) alpine ponds" for $8 million. This acreage is actually the Saddleback Mountain Ski area and surrounding lakes and forest, but that isn't mentioned, skiing being a liability rather than an asset to the likely use of this land, a thirteen-square-mile "kingdom" for either a condominium development or a giant single home.

In the face of such pressures, the challenge is to preserve a wild trail and a wild forest. The trail desperately needs protectors, people who dream of wild areas also being available for their children, grandchildren, and future generations forever.

BOB CUMMINGS covered environmental affairs for the *Portland Press Herald* and the *Maine Sunday Telegram* for twenty-five years. After retiring a decade ago, he spent a spring, summer, and early fall walking most of the Appalachian Trail from Springer Mountain in Georgia, north to Katahdin in Maine. He is also president of the Phippsburg Land Trust, which he helped found twenty-five years ago, and a director of the Maine Appalachian Trail Land Trust. He oversees the maintenance of 60 miles of the Appalachian Trail and edits newsletters for the Maine Appalachian Trail Club and the Maine Chapter, Appalachian Mountain Club. A Maine native, he was born in Bath and currently lives in Phippsburg.

HIKING ON BIGELOW

the sound of the mountain
humming under my feet
melting through late winter ice
rising from speckled ledge
and swelling in the buds of large birches

picking up tempo
my bones feel the sound
I breathe it in
        as streams drum out its voice
and light-flecked patterns dance along rushing water

the sound is aching
the sound is stone coming to life
the sound is the color of radiance
        and of dark massive angles

it is a roar in my mind

—Karin R. Tilberg, 1988–89

KARIN R. TILBERG's bio can be found on page 34.

My home and studio overlook the Dead River in the shadow of the Bigelow Range just upstream from Flagstaff Lake. The river, lake, and mountains figure prominently in my paintings, for they figure prominently in my life. I keep journals of weather, wildlife, and seasons; I record ice out, arrival of the first wood ducks, return of the phoebe, a killing frost. In late winter I snowshoe on the river following critter tracks; in summer we canoe and fish and picnic on the lake. I know where to find mayflowers and beaver houses and otter slides. I take photographs, make sketches, splash watercolors, and haul my French easel out in the boat when the black flies are too brutal on shore. The vanishing backwoods landscape of Maine has long been a major concern of my paintings, and here in my own neck of the woods, I have the great good fortune to enjoy a unique intimacy with my subject.

MARGUERITE ROBICHAUX lives and works in her studio in the woods of Maine. She also spends time painting in southern Louisiana where she grew up. She received her M.F.A. from Louisiana State University and first came to Maine while a student. Her paintings are included in the collections of the New Orleans Museum of Art, the Portland Museum of Art, the Farnsworth Museum, the Ogunquit Museum of American Art, Colby and Bates Colleges, as well as many private and corporate collections. She is represented by Pucker Gallery in Boston and Sylvia Schmidt Gallery in New Orleans.

EAST TO BIGELOW

Marguerite Robichaux

13¹/₄ x 24 inches, etching, aquatint

If We Do Not Have Wilderness. . . .

Jon Lund

My most remote wilderness experience took place on a canoe and fishing trip on a Quebec river that empties into the Gulf of St. Lawrence. We drove a hundred miles north from the Canadian coast, then continued north by floatplane another hundred miles into the backcountry. We landed on a headwater lake and unloaded our gear and canoes, confirmed our rendezvous plan with the pilot, and watched the plane take off and disappear. We were two hundred miles from civilization; if something went wrong, we would have to solve the problem ourselves.

For the better part of a week, we didn't see any sign of the hand of man, not a campsite, nor a sign of firewood-cutting among the dwarf spruce trees and brush, nor even a boot-print on the sandy shore. Only caribou tracks. Eventually we observed a silvery scrape mark on an underwater rock where an aluminum craft had dragged, but we didn't see another human being until the floatplane appeared in the sky at our rendezvous point.

We were in what I would fairly call wilderness.

We don't have much by way of wilderness in the Northeast. Baxter State Park and the Allagash Wilderness Waterway come immediately to mind, as does the St. John River canoe trip. Purists chafe at the pressures of overuse and consequent careful regulation of activities at Baxter, and point out that on the Allagash Wilderness Waterway, a short walk beyond the campsite outhouse usually offers the view of a vast clearcut.

More recently, our party was standing at the summit of Katahdin in Baxter State Park, catching our breath. We had crossed the Knife Edge and the Tableland lay ahead. The panorama of lakes and forestland was stretched out below us. We stood beside the cairn that marks the peak, admiring the vastness and beauty that lay below.

A few feet away, a young man took out a cell phone and proceeded to make a call and asked the party at the other end to guess where he was calling from. When he finished his call, I approached him and pointed out that using a cell phone was against park regulations. He replied that he was unaware of the regulation and apologized and put the phone away in his daypack.

On another Baxter Park trip, our party had made the trek into Russell Pond, where we were staying at the bunkhouse. Russell Pond is one of my favorite places in Baxter State Park because of its remoteness and beauty. To get there, a hiker has to walk at least eight miles along old woods roads and trails carrying food, clothing, cooking utensils, sleeping bags, and other camping needs.

In the morning, as we assembled for breakfast, one member of our group, who had been listening on the earphone of his tiny radio, gave us a summary of the morning news. No one pointed out that use of the radio was against Park rules, but the subject was changed quickly to the plans for the morning's activities, and the morning's news was soon forgotten.

These two unconnected events have weighed on my mind as I have pondered the meaning of wilderness. To me, wilderness is not a place, a scene, or a landscape, but a state of mind that forms as a human reacts to the totality of his surroundings.

To an urban dweller unaccustomed to scenery without vehicular traffic, buildings, asphalt, and the noise that accompanies those artifacts, a quiet moment on the shore of an undeveloped lake where no other humans are in sight may well convey the impression of wilderness even though he just stepped out of his car and will return to the highway in a matter of minutes.

To the experienced backwoods traveler, however, something more is required to convey that impression of wilderness. In addition to untrammeled scenery, a certain separation from the complexities that mark modern life is often required. Thus the jarring note of a hiker making a superfluous call on his cell phone impaired for a moment the sense of wilderness, as did our friend who regaled his party with the morning news that no one wanted to hear. The physical surroundings were unchanged, but the intrusion of modern technology bringing in the outside world shattered the spell of wilderness.

In the United States, we have provided ourselves with easy and effortless transportation, surrounded ourselves with instant communication, and filled our ears with constant talk and musical entertainment to the point where many people feel uneasy if they find themselves alone, and in silence.

Critics of the idea of establishing or preserving wilderness areas argue that there are no longer wilderness areas in Maine where man has not left his mark. Without conceding the accuracy of their argument, the appropriate response is that the critics' argument is irrelevant. While there are but few places in our state that have not felt the bite of the logger's axe and saw, natural balance can be achieved. With sufficient time and patience, nature will re-assert itself.

We are rapidly losing the tracts of undeveloped forests where we can enjoy solitude and quiet, losing to the real estate developers, liquidation foresters, and road-builders. Experience tells us that once built, roads are rarely closed and returned to forest growth. We are losing the peace of our lakes, spoiled by high-speed motor boats and jet-skis in summer and snowmobiles in winter. As the noise and clutter of mechanization and technology press upon us, it becomes doubly important that we establish and protect wilderness areas as a place of peace and quiet, a sanctuary not only for wildlife, but also for humans.

If we don't have wilderness, we won't know what our land is like where humans have not altered it. If we do not have wilderness we won't know how we can live without internal combustion engines, radios, and telephones. If we do not have wilderness, we won't know the sounds of silence, broken only by the talk of the trees and the waves, the hoot of the owl, cry of the osprey, and call of the loon.

JON LUND is publisher of *The Maine Sportsman,* for which he writes a monthly column. A former Maine Attorney General, he served in both the state senate and house, where he was outspoken in his support of conservation issues. He attended Augusta public schools, graduated from Bowdoin College and Harvard Law School, and practiced law in Augusta. He is a past president of the Natural Resources Council of Maine, the Maine League of Conservation Voters, and the Maine Civil Liberties Union. An active outdoorsman, his interests include hunting and fishing, sailing, canoeing, and cross-country skiing.

Denizen of mature forests and most arboreal of the weasels, the pine marten thrives only where true wilderness conditions, or land carefully managed as wildlands, exist. Hunter of mice and voles along the forest floor, the marten is also an able climber and quick enough to give a squirrel a run for its money in the tree-tops. It is the embodiment of wildness because unlike more adaptable creatures, the marten will simply not tolerate any other condition.

JERRY STELMOK is a Maine native who has enjoyed the woods and waters of his native state most of his life. It was not until canoe trips in Labrador in the 1980s and '90s that he was able to fully appreciate the unique sensual and spiritual experiences true wilderness can impart on a traveler. Professionally, Stelmok builds traditional wood-and-canvas canoes, many models designed for extensive wilderness trips. He also teaches the craft, has written several books on the subject, and when he is not building, he enjoys paddling, hunting, fishing, snowshoeing, and painting. He lives in Atkinson.

Pine Marten

Jerry Stelmok

A FOREST RESERVE SYSTEM IN MAINE

Malcolm L. Hunter, Jr.

Maine's forests are inherently areas of great natural diversity. Sandwiched between two major forest regions, the boreal spruce-fir forests to the north and the temperate deciduous forests to the south, our forests are at an ecological crossroads that draws its flora and fauna from two directions. Moreover, Maine's rugged and varied terrain provides a mosaic of environments—wind-swept mountain tops, flooded river bottoms, sandy plains of glacial sediments, deep organic soils, and coastal outcroppings of granite—that all have their special associations of plants and animals that comprise the forest ecosystems of Maine. When you look closely you soon realize that there are many types of forests in Maine; to see our forests as just hardwood forest, softwood forest, or mixed forest is to take a very myopic view.

The diversity of Maine's forests is multiplied enormously if you consider the thousands of forms of life that create each forest ecosystem. Some of these are as conspicuous and well known as moose and oaks, but a large majority are of microscopic size and are hardly ever seen. Tiny invertebrates, fungi, and bacteria exist by the millions in every handful of soil. Although very inconspicuous, these species are ultimately just as important as the moose and oaks because without them, and the role they play in providing a nutrient-rich, aerated soil, there would be no forest.

Unfortunately, we know incredibly little about the smaller forms of life in our forest. Consider the fact that a spider biologist, Dan Jennings of the U.S. Forest Service, spent several summers collecting spiders in one type of Maine forest and discovered six species that were new to science. And spiders are very conspicuous and easy to identify compared to most creatures.

Because most living things are so inconspicuous and poorly known it would be impossible to develop individual conservation schemes for each of them, species by species, the way we do for bald eagles and white-tailed deer. The only practical way to preserve populations of all these species, and the ecosystems they comprise, is to set aside representative examples of the various types of Maine forest in a system of forest reserves as we have begun to do.

The rationale for establishing such a forest reserve system extends far beyond maintaining the biological diversity of Maine's forests. Reserves provide critically needed control areas for forest research, natural seed stocks for forest geneticists, and attractive areas for limited recreation. For example, our understanding of the spruce budworm's impact on forest ecology has been substantially improved by research in Baxter State Park where there was no budworm spraying.

So ecological reserves provide many values, but are they wilderness? And conversely, does a wilderness serve as an ecological reserve? Both are sizable tracts of land and waters where the hand of humanity is minimized, and thus they have a great deal in common. The difference is one of emphasis. For ecological reserves, maintaining an array of first-class examples of ecosystems well distributed around the state is paramount. Some of these may be quite modest in size and have no special recreational amenities, such as dramatic vistas. In wilderness areas, recreation comes first, and the best examples are large stretches where a person can travel for days enjoying nature at its most magnificent.

To illustrate this point more explicitly, imagine presenting Maine to a wilderness advocate and an ecological-reserve advocate as a clean slate, before human habitation, and asking them each to identify two million acres to be set aside before the people arrived. I bet the wilderness advocate would select two large tracts, one around Katahdin and the nearby rivers and one along the coast, centered on Mount Desert Island. The ecological-reserve advocate would probably choose both of these places too, but I expect that at least a million acres would be held back to create a dozen or more modest-sized reserves, perhaps one reaching from Mt. Agamenticus to some coastal beaches and salt marshes, perhaps another centered on one of our outstanding peatland complexes. These differences are not trivial, but under both scenarios we would maintain an important segment of Maine's natural heritage and the opportunity to enjoy it.

Note: This essay was modified, notably with addition of the last two paragraphs, from one that originally appeared in Maine Audubon's *Habitat* 2(8):34 and is reprinted here with permission.

MALCOLM "MAC" HUNTER, JR., is the Libra Professor of Conservation Biology in the Department of Wildlife Ecology at the University of Maine. A native of Damariscotta, he earned his B. S. at the University of Maine and then went to Oxford University where he received a Ph.D. He has pursued research on a wide range of organisms and ecosystems—birds, amphibians, plants, mammals, lakes, peatlands, grasslands, and especially forests—and produced five books on forest biodiversity, conservation biology, and herpetology. His interests are also geographically broad: he has worked in over twenty-five countries, mainly in Africa and the Himalayas.

THE HARRIER

The mist disperses and lifts from the field
in the whitest feathers, feathers dropped, perhaps,
from the harrier quartering
over the brown grass, which already
is beginning to green. I think
about angels, I wonder
if <u>they</u> ever catch mice? Everything
is here to accept this morning, to take in,
to applaud: the hawk's wide, predatory
circles, sunlight coming and going, cloud shadows
constantly shifting, a toss of rain, and then
the line of bare poplars standing ghostly
under the slope in a streak
of sudden light (but we know
there are buds on those pale twigs) and the veils
of moisture that hang in the air,
visible . . . invisible . . . making the hills soft,
and distant, and mildly blue, and changeable,
like the breath in my body, in
and then out . . . in and then out . . .
as long as it will.

—Kate Barnes

KATE BARNES, Maine's first poet laureate, lives on a farm in
Appleton that raises blueberries and hay. Her parents were the
Maine writers Elizabeth Coatsworth and Henry Beston. Her
first book of poetry, *Where the Deer Were,* came out with David
R. Godine, Inc. in 1995. A second book of poems, *Kneeling
Orion,* is expected for next year.

Birds of the Forest Woods

Margaret Campbell

MARGARET CAMPBELL, graphic designer and illustrator, lives and works in her studio in Bowdoinham, surrounded by woods and fields. She has worked in advertising and illustration for *Maine Times* for ten years, while also doing freelance projects for other regional newspapers and colleges. She spent four years at Maine Audubon Society designing and developing the organization's journal, *Habitat,* and other environmental education materials. Margaret began her art studies at the High School of Art and Design in Manhattan and has a Bachelor of Fine Arts degree from Pratt Institute in Brooklyn. She has an affinity for nature, birds, and weather.

TREE

Susan Hand Shetterly

The house I live in sits at the edge of a small field surrounded by trees. They are mostly softwoods—white pines and red spruces, northern white cedars, balsam firs, hemlocks, and two or three tamaracks. The white pines, which I am told were saplings the year Lincoln delivered his second inaugural, are especially tall. They cast shadows across the field. They reach up straight and close together like a quiver of gigantic arrows, a memory of trees before they bore the king's mark, before they were felled to hold aloft the sails of an empire.

On the other side of the town road, the land has been clear-cut. Down at the marsh behind my house, the land's been over-cut, the brush and broken trees that are left, an impenetrable thicket of waste. On my land nothing has been cut for a long, long time, except to make this little clearing.

A friend once asked me if the big trees and the tiny field made me feel hemmed in. I don't think so, I told him. I wasn't sure why.

Now I believe it is because an old dead pine about sixty feet tall points above a copse of cedars and firs. It stands south of the kitchen windows. I see it every time I look outside. Over the years, it has trained my vision upward, into the open sky and the weather.

Its long snags once stretched to the west. Most of them have fallen, and it looks less like a fish's backbone and ribs and more like a thrust of index finger—fierce and stark. While the other trees swing their branches in a wind—and in a gale, they thrash—the old pine offers only a brittle tremor. When snow clings in drifts to the other trees, the old tree accepts a mere cup of it, stuck between the silvered trunk and a stub.

Every day I meet it. It is always spare, true, and my eyes follow its directive into the sky. One could say it refuses adornment and disapproves of dancing, that it is an alarming old Calvinist—a most terribly alive dead tree.

And one could say it's a fine bird perch. It has, in fact, been a generous teacher, showing me something about the birds who live in these woods, who come to this field.

As I write this, a flicker has latched itself to the tree. I watch the bird dart its head around to one side and shout "wicka-wicka-wicka," and fly off. An hour ago, two resident pileated woodpeckers shimmied up the tree. They were yelling "kuk-kuk-kuk-kuk," a brash call, much like the flicker's. But if you hear the calls one after the other—which my tree offers—an undertone of complaint reveals itself in the flicker's; the pileated sound is big and confident.

Last February a white-winged crossbill, a male, stood at the top of the tree and sang in a sharp twitter. The temperature was dropping every night, and here was this bird in the morning claiming territory, as if he thought he had a nest somewhere. I read about crossbills, and learned that he did indeed have a nest. Probably on a spruce, probably about ten feet up, and out on a branch. But I never found it. And I never saw his mate. He sang from the old tree every day for four cold weeks.

A band of crows flew down late last winter after the crossbill left. They gorged themselves on the cracked corn I throw out in the field for the turkeys. Their sentinel took its solitary place on one of the lower snags of the tree. A silent bird, it kept an eye out as the others jabbed in the melting snow. Spring came on, and the sentinel watched the others shout and frolic; sometimes they scooted on their sides in the slush, jumped up and walked around each other with bowlegged swaggers, or they slapped wet snow on themselves with their wings as if it were water.

One day the flock and the sentinel and the snow disappeared. The ground was muddy, the little pond in the field was overflowing, and whispered crow talk issued from somewhere in the woods behind the old tree. It sounded like a conversation between two.

In a week, the pair showed itself. The birds perched in a red maple as it flowered. They sat wing to wing, nuzzling each other's heads and backs with their beaks.

Robins flew in but didn't stay. White-throated sparrows sang, but the songs stopped. The mourning doves left. Crows pillage other birds' nests, and one day I found a naked half-eaten squab on the driveway.

As spring turned to early summer, a single crow perched on a stub of the old tree, its wings held like hunched shoulders. The body language looked to me as if the bird felt ill-tempered, worn out. Then a few weeks of fledgling crow-scream bothered the place before the woods fell silent, the crows disappeared, and the robins came back. A big red-breasted male claimed the top of the old tree. A white-throated sparrow family found a spot to nest somewhere on the ground in the cedar brush near its base, and the male sang its lovely plainsong. A blue-headed vireo sang from tree to tree all around the green field.

When I bought thirty goldfish at the pet store in Ellsworth one summer, I slipped them into the pond at the bottom of the field, and invited everyone who stopped in to come down and sit with me to watch fish like jewels swim among the lily pads. I couldn't get over how beautiful they were. They grew quickly. They survived a winter under the ice.

The next summer, a kingfisher flew in to study them from the old tree. It was a female, with a belt of rust-colored feathers across her chest. I'd hear her rattling call, drop whatever I was doing, sprint as fast as I could to the pond, shouting to scare the bird off. Sometimes I arrived in time to see her splash between the lilies. She would shoot out of the water with a bright orange glint at her beak and fly back to her perch on the old tree. Before my eyes she swallowed my gorgeous fish. One by one. By summer's end, she had eaten them all.

Mourning doves, the males with a wash of pink on their breasts, often perch on the tree, gray on gray, while the sky beyond them turns rosy on late summer evenings. Slowly, as the light leaves, the doves begin to look more like the branch stubs. Just at the moment when I can no longer distinguish them from the tree itself, they take off to safer roosts.

A forester who is a friend came by last week to talk about cutting some fir to let light in for the young white pines. He looked across the field and said, "Nice tree," and I looked around to find the one he was talking about.

"Which one?" I asked him.

"The dead pine," he said.

"Since when do foresters like dead trees?"

"We had a dead elm in our yard when our kids were small," he said. "We got all sorts of birds coming to it."

"Like what?" I asked.

"It had a hole where a limb had fallen off, and one summer pileated woodpeckers nested in it. It drew birds all year long—swallows, robins, evening grosbeaks. When it collapsed, we were pretty disappointed."

"That old pine will be here," I told him, "probably forever."

He smiled. "You can't go out and buy one like it . . . perches, beetle larvae, ants—good stuff."

After he left, I worried. Sure, my tree grew thinner and more insistently pointed every year, but it never occurred to me that it might fall. I bushwhacked through the clumps of wet fir and cedar to the old tree's base to get a closer look. I needed to be sure that it was sturdily planted. That it was okay. There, in the gloom of the thick woods, I saw my tree up close for the first time, and a life I hadn't known about—a past I hadn't been curious enough to ask about—presented itself no more than a few inches from my face.

Down the trunk ran a lightning scar. It was deep and wide. The tree had been burned to the heartwood, which was pitted and grooved and dark. To mend itself, it had grown a thick, smooth, milky-white ridge of living tissue on either side of the scar. But with that strike, its trunk had lost a third of its bark. When had this happened? Maybe fifty years ago. Maybe more. I looked around at the litter on the ground, the stuff the tree has been dropping for years: branches the size of ribs and tusks, wrinkled sheets of bark as tough as elephant knees. At the base was a large hole and I stuck my hand in, reached up, and found no end to it.

Leaning against the damaged trunk, I closed my eyes and

breathed in the smell of rotting wood. Then I looked up and saw that this trunk was not the original trunk. The original was a few feet above my head, stunted, withered.

When my tree was a mere adolescent, years before the lightning strike, a pine weevil, a beetle with spotted, dull-brown wing coverts, had laid its eggs in the terminal shoot, just below the terminal bud, which is the place where a tree grows. No tree grows from the base. Carve your initials into a sapling and they will be at the same height as long as the tree stands. The part that reaches farther into the sky every year is the bud, and it is that which a weevil smaller than a shelled peanut killed on my tree. But, slowly—because it had no intention of dying—the tree reached one of its main branches upward to take the place of the dead trunk, fighting gravity's heavy tug as it transformed its horizontal into vertical. It converted that branch to a new trunk and kept on growing, and the branch grew thick. From it reached many side branches, and for years this crippled tree thrived. Until lightning scalded it. And long-horned beetles bored holes into the dead wood. They laid eggs. The larvae hatched and crawled around in the heartwood and pupated and emerged flying and laid more eggs in the tree. Carpenter ants found the bark loosened by the long-horns. They made tunnels under it and what fell from beneath the bark was frass—which means insect dung—and kerf—which means sawdust.

Now great piles of frass and kerf lie in wet mounds around the base. Pileated woodpecker holes pit the trunk and the big branch that became the trunk as the birds pry the tree apart searching for the larvae of the long-horns and for the ants.

Finally, I can't help but see that my tree is braced between a cedar and a fir. Like nurses in end-of-life care, they hold it aloft.

I find myself getting up in the dark now to stand by the south windows down in the kitchen, to look into the sky for the tree, to make sure it's there. I've never seen a bird on it at night, but it may be at its most dramatic then—emphatic—with the clouds skimming in back of it.

Sometimes, as I stand there, I see the moon emerge from behind a cloud to glaze my old tree in clean, cold light.

SUSAN HAND SHETTERLY lives in Surry. She teaches, and writes narrative essays, children's books, short fiction, and articles. She has received two grants from the Maine Arts Commission, a grant from the National Endowment for the Arts, and commendations for her writing for children in the fields of science and social studies. She has been a writer-in-residence at the University of Maine at Orono and a resident at Yaddo.

Wilderness in Time Future

John Cole

Time present is indeed time future, and it portends the greatest change in Maine character since the first Indian attacks along the Kennebec River almost 400 years ago.

Within the past five years, nearly 30 percent, or six million acres, of Maine's land base has been sold, and parts of that have already been resold. And this trend is accelerating even as you read. The major landholders, the pulp and paper companies whose lobbyists once held court at the old Augusta House next to Maine's capitol building, are taking their leave. The pine and spruce and hardwoods that grow so slowly in Maine's unforgiving winters are no longer producing the returns they once did. The pulp and paper and timber industries are moving south, far south to the vast wilderness of the Amazon Basin where the same trees grow more than twice as fast and the labor needed for harvest costs half as much as it does in North America.

These are today's realities. They will not change that much in time future. As much as worthy institutions like The Nature Conservancy and the Natural Resources Council of Maine work to acquire conservation easements or outright ownership, they and their counterpart agencies don't have the unlimited resources to keep up with the masses of Maine woodland put on the block.

Well aware of this accelerating trend, RESTORE: The North Woods, with its Maine office in Hallowell, keeps working on its plan for its Maine Woods National Park and Preserve, a 3.2-million-acre parcel of Maine North Woods that would enclose Baxter State Park and part of the Allagash Wilderness Waterway, and stretch west across Maine's middle from the Upper Sebois

River Gorge to the ponds on the Quebec border that are the source of the St. John River.

As you might have guessed, the plan is energetically opposed by those with development plans for the last and largest wildland in the Northeast. The naysayers are offset by scores of prominent national supporters who should have some clout when it comes to activating the park's enabling legislation in Congress.

But will this stunning proposal evolve to reality within the next ten or fifteen years? It's too close to call. What's needed is an egregiously blatant wildlands developer who may make a quick buck, but who will do it so wantonly that he alerts all of us to the need for wildlands protection as sturdy and eternal as a national park. I'll give you six to five that just such a developer will be a presence in Maine's time future.

There is a part of me that hopes for just such a desecration, only because it could energize a spirited reaction that will iden-tify a part of Maine that all of us will unite to designate a true wilderness, a lonely and sacrosanct region of solitude and, if you will, nonmanagement. As the Beatles wrote, just "let it be."

Take the top of Maine, the land that projects north to Quebec above the Allagash and reaches the border at Escourt Station and Riviere-Bleue. This is the region where most wild wolf sightings originate. Too often, they end in tragedy, for if a wild wolf is truly identified, it is, in defiance of the law, shot and killed and then argued over at its autopsy. This is also where most mountain lions are seen, shadowy predators leaving their large paw prints in wet snow. I like to think, and do so stubbornly, that these wildest of creatures are there, that both the wolf and mountain lion patrol what they see as wilderness, what they see as their place to be.

Although we may not always realize it, we need to know such places exist, not in dreams but in reality. For the concept of wilderness, a space of the wild, is a dimension as important to our well-being as the air itself. We are forever enriched and sus-tained by the certain knowledge that wilderness exists, not in our history books, but as our neighbor just north of the Allagash. This is what we must hope and pray Maine's uncertain future holds.

There is, however, one certainty: real estate prices will continue to increase. Not one square foot of Maine land, on the coast or deep in the forest, will cost less in time future than it does in time present.

The demands on what is, after all, a finite supply are simply too inexorable. From everywhere across its borders, Maine is perceived as secure, a place where old-time verities apply, a place where children are the beneficiaries of a human-scale environment, a place where the truth is still spoken.

Let us pray that as they have since time's beginning, the sea and the woods will remain Maine's most palpable presences, defining the state's eternal character in ways we have yet to fully comprehend. For this state is, as its very name proclaims, a great stretch of land along a vast expanse of sea.

This shall never change, not in the next decade or the next millennia.

Note: This essay is adapted from an article that originally appeared in the January 2003 issue of *Down East* magazine.

JOHN N. COLE was one of Maine's most distinguished journalists and writers. After almost a half century in the newspaper business, he died of cancer on January 8, 2003, just seven weeks short of his eightieth birthday. Cole rose to prominence as editor of *Maine Times*, a groundbreaking advocacy newspaper that he co-founded in late 1968. He grew up on Long Island, New York, and left Yale University to serve in the Army Air Corps during World War II. He became a much-decorated airman for flying combat missions over Europe. After graduating from Yale, he tried his hand at commercial fishing off Long Island and then moved to Maine in the early '50s. He became the editor at newspapers in Kennebunk and Bath/Brunswick. In 1968 he founded the *Maine Times* with Peter Cox, and later he created the *World Paper*. Cole was a prolific writer (with thirteen books to his credit), a visionary of the post-industrial world, and the recipient of many prestigious awards.

I have spent a lifetime exploring the brooks and hills in the backwoods of my home state. I have spent a career being a voice in the wilderness for protection and restoration of the special places in Maine that have touched me profoundly. However, it is through my photography of Maine's wild landscapes—some grand, some intimate—that I have felt most blessed. The eye of the camera has helped me to see worlds that I otherwise would have walked over or driven by. This image of sunrise at Spencer Pond, deep in the Maine woods, is a good example. I reached this spot at twilight in late July and decided to camp nearby. At daybreak the sun was backlighting a narrow peninsula of trees and a thin cloud of golden mist floating above the water. The symmetry of Little Spencer Mountain reflected in the pond was world-class. Though I was alone, I hope I was able to capture and share through my photo of the scene a sense of that brief, sublime moment. Please remember it with me. Then take action to ensure that a hundred years from now, someone not yet born will be able to have their own wilderness experience at sunrise on a remote Maine lake.

JYM ST. PIERRE is Maine director of RESTORE: The North Woods. After earning degrees in philosophy and natural resources from the University of Maine, he worked for the Maine Department of Conservation, the Sierra Club, and The Wilderness Society. He has been active in many conservation organizations, including the Maine League of Conservation Voters, Citizens to Protect the Allagash, The Nature Conservancy Maine Chapter, the Natural Resources Council of Maine, Maine Woods Trust, Kennebec Land Trust, Friends of Baxter State Park, and Readfield Conservation Commission. He enjoys taking photos and collecting books. He lives in Readfield with his wife and two sons.

LITTLE SPENCER MOUNTAIN

Jym St. Pierre

WILDNESS AND WILDERNESS
A Northeastern Perspective

Lloyd C. Irland

Since the days of Thoreau, those of us living in the Northeastern region (New England, New York, New Jersey, and Pennsylvania) have appreciated wild forest landscapes.* We pushed for state forests and parks as early as the 1880s, with the citizen-led effort to create the Adirondack Park. Local citizens pressed for federal acquisition of land in the White Mountain National Forest. Maine contains a splendid example of a privately created wilderness—Baxter State Park. Today, about 12 percent of the region's forest land is publicly owned.

The forest has regrown so completely that few hikers realize that many a trailside vista was once farmed or abusively cut, and often burned. Regionwide, 17 million acres of cleared land returned to forest from 1909 to 1992—an area equal to Maine's present forest area. The few remaining scraps of true virgin forest are mostly outside the region's large, formally designated wilderness areas. Supportive as they have been of public lands, Northeasterners have not seen fit, outside of the Adirondacks, to allocate large areas of public land to wilderness preservation. This is partly because motorized river and trail uses are well established and vigorously defended almost everywhere.

The boundaries of the wild forest are difficult to define, but they surround a range of forest lands in public and conservation ownership whose primary objective is the maintenance of natural conditions. Large acreages of the wild forest are devoted to such uses as watershed protection, but these lands may be available for limited timber cutting, so they fit no rigid definition of wilderness. Tiny parcels owned as greenspace or preserves by towns and nonprofit groups are also part of the wild forest. We could also add more than a million backcountry acres in the national forests, fish and game lands, state parks, and private non-profit reservations that will retain a generally unmanaged character. This total of, say, 5 million acres comes to about 5 percent of the region's land area. Of this, only a fraction is true designated wilderness. This is well below the Brundtland Commission's suggestion for 12 percent in reserves.★★

Wild forests provide many scientific, economic, cultural, and ethical values. Large portions of the wild forest were created for utilitarian purposes—to preserve game, fish, and clean water supplies or to conserve channel storage and prevent flood plain encroachment. Protecting water supplies was a major argument for federal acquisition of the White Mountain National Forest and for creating the Adirondack Park. Recreation, birdwatching, and open space values have been high on the list of objectives in virtually every instance. The pure "preservation" motive, best expressed by Baxter State Park, is also seen in dozens of tiny parcels of woods and marsh held by The Nature Conservancy, other private nonprofit groups, and some private owners. Aside from direct ownership of public land, a totally unexpected development of the late 1990s has been the dramatic increase in the use of conservation easements to "immunize" wildlands against subdivision and development and to capture for the future some values of the wild forest. In many projects, opportunities have been taken to preserve outstanding parcels or stretches of lake—and riverfront. But preservation is not the primary objective of these easements.

Outside the Adirondacks, restrictive categories of wilderness are relatively new to the Northeast and, other than the "forever wild" of Baxter State Park, cover a small area. Much of the 5-million-acre "wild forest" is open to motorized canoes, RVs, and snowmobiles. Wilderness lakes are reached by aircraft. Motorized woods users have enormous political clout; their organized opposition accounts in large part for the minimal acreage of public land designated as wilderness here. It is plain that true wilderness in the region is a chimera without some way of reducing and managing the impacts of motorization. Whether this is even possible is uncertain. The bitter fights over access to the Allagash Wilderness Waterway are but one example. Additional designations of "wilderness" will not be able to provide visitors with solitude unless this issue can be confronted.

I believe that a sensible conservation program for the region has two parts: land acquisition and cooperative landscape management on private land. First, I would attempt to increase the acreage in the Northeast's publicly owned wild forest by 50 percent by the year 2020—from 5 to 7.5 million acres. A large part of this increase should be in true wilderness. This would still be only 7.5 percent of the region's land, well below the Brundtland recommendations. The effort should focus on bolstering existing large and remote publicly owned areas, especially those with key wildlife values, but would also involve private groups acquiring small, key parcels. An enlarged wild forest would be a prize bequest for this generation to pass to the future. While there are advocates of single, large reserves, I think a case can be made for a more dispersed approach which would represent a greater diversity of ecosystems.

But public wildlands will not be enough. I propose establishing designated Landscape Management Areas (LMAs). Within these, targeted public support would be provided for private landowners voluntarily implementing long rotations, using related "New Forestry" practices, using expanded stream and trail protection, and giving up development rights. At the core of each LMA might be an area of true "wilderness." The design details do not concern us here. The concept is that there are innovative ways to serve long-term land protection goals that fit economic, social, and biological realities of this diverse region. The idea builds on an earlier proposal by Charles Foster of Harvard for "Legacy Forests." The concept is not merely to obtain development rights on narrow buffer zones adjacent to public land units. Rather, it is an effort to secure habitat and wilderness values over naturally meaningful areas, perhaps quite large in size. Private lands in the LMAs are not included in my 7.5-million-acre proposed total.

Adding acres to the region's public estate will not be the best solution in every area. Also, outright acquisition may not be cost effective or politically feasible. States will be in the lead in this region, but the fiscal and political climate do not appear favorable for large-scale land acquisition. For example, Maine's previous governor stated his opposition to RESTORE: The North Woods' National Park proposal. Further, Maine's timber inventory situation leaves little, if any, room for trade-offs at present. It would seem wise to consider new approaches. A much richer and more wide-ranging program of policy design, public education, and advocacy will be needed on the part of the wilderness community. A proposals for a 5-million-acre Thoreau National Reserve has also been offered. Also, a coalition of Northeastern groups has identified ten major wildland areas regionwide for conservation efforts. I would also add that the past lack of attention paid to Southern Maine needs to end.

Thoughtful scientists and citizens realize that the region's heritage of wildness, its wildlife habitat and biodiversity values, and its traditions of public recreational uses cannot be preserved by designated public wilderness areas alone. For this reason, wilderness must be seen as an essential element in a broader effort designed to retain wildness, biodiversity, and public access over larger landscapes. This process could be promoted through designated Landscape Management Areas. More sensitive landscape management of large public forest units and industrial properties can provide many of the values of the wild forest over a much wider area (see, for example, Maine Council on Sustainable Forest Management 1996). We need to develop more innovative ways to secure the protection of wildlands for the future.

A longer view is needed. The existing National Wilderness Preservation System wasn't built in a day. A long-term program focused on practical means of protecting wildness, instead of immediate designations of huge wilderness areas, will be unsatisfying to many wilderness activists. But the perfect can be the enemy of the good. I believe this proposal builds on regional traditions, recognizes financial and political realities, and would deliver major benefits. This generation's bequest of wildness to the future is being shaped now. I think these ideas deserve the support of the region's wilderness community.

* Portions of this essay and references can be found in *Wilderness Economics and Policy* (1979) and *The Northeast's Changing Forests* (Harvard Forest, 1999) by the author.
** The Brundtland Commission was a worldwide commission on sustainable development that issued a widely read report in 1987.

LLOYD IRLAND is president of The Irland Group, a forest economics and marketing consulting firm in Winthrop. The firm provides resources analysis, cost and economic studies, and market research to private clients, as well as evaluation and policy analyses for government agencies. Much of the firm's work is concentrated in the northern tier states from Minnesota to Maine and in adjacent Canadian provinces. Irland served as an associate economist for the USDA Forest Service, assistant professor at the Yale School of Forestry and Environmental Studies, and as state economist for Maine before forming The Irland Group in 1987.

LYNX AND GRAY JAY

Dean Bennett

The seldom-seen, secretive lynx symbolizes the wildness and mystique of the North Woods. The curious, pesky gray jay, on the other hand, is well known to those who visit the region. We have an obligation to protect the rare and commonplace in our woods—the top predators and the plants and animals beneath them in the web of life.

Note: This drawing has appeared in *Allagash: Maine's Wild and Scenic River* (Camden, Maine: Down East Books, 1994).

DEAN B. BENNETT, born and raised in western Maine, is professor emeritus at the University of Maine at Farmington. Much of his professional life has been devoted to teaching and writing in the fields of science and environmental education, natural history, and human relationships with nature, and to advocacy work in wilderness protection. His books include *Maine's Natural Heritage, Allagash: Maine's Wild and Scenic River, The Forgotten Nature of New England,* and *The Wilderness from Chamberlain Farm.* When he and his wife, Sheila, aren't canoeing and hiking, they enjoy the woods and bogs surrounding their Mt. Vernon home.

CARVING WILDERNESS OUT OF CIVILIZATION

Dean Bennett

I had stared in disbelief at what I'd seen. Now, inside, I reached over and rested the palm of my hand on the cold steel lever, still smooth and polished after so many years. I curled my fingers around it and pulled. Immediately, hissing coughs broke the stillness, growing more rapid and louder. Wisps of steam passed by outside, just catching the sunlight before they dissolved into the cool air. I thought I detected a smell of burning oil. Then the lever vibrated with the anticipated sounds of steel on steel grinding for traction, and I heard the inevitable clunking of the couplings dominoing off into the distance behind me. Ahead through the trees, I could glimpse the lake shimmering in the early afternoon sun, but the trees were not moving past me as they should have been.

For a fleeting moment of passing fancy, it had been easy to imagine that the lever I gripped set in motion the ninety tons of iron surrounding me. But nearly three-quarters of a century had passed since the firing up of engine No. 2 for its run on the Eagle Lake and West Branch Railroad. Now the giant locomotive sat quietly rusting away in a clearing of enclosing spruce, fir, yellow birch, and other northern hardwoods. The engine had been brought here in 1928 in pieces and put into operation hauling pulpwood over a thirteen-mile railroad cut out of the Allagash wildlands. Five years later it fell victim to the Great Depression and was abandoned here near the shore of Eagle Lake.

If I had been able to live out my fantasy and drive the locomotive just a few feet ahead, I would have passed right over the site of another technological advance in log hauling established here—the half-mile-long Tramway. Predating the railroad by twenty years, this conveyor of long logs between Eagle and Chamberlain Lakes was an extraordinary mechanical innovation for getting wood out of the Allagash region. In five years, it moved a hundred million feet of lumber, and in the course of doing so, it must have raised doubts in men's minds about the future of horses and oxen in the woods. Technology, as we all know, moves on, constantly outstripping itself, and by 1907 the Tramway was obsolete. Today, visitors to this place can still see the 6,000-foot cable with its attached iron log-holding cradles rusting on the ground in the dark shade of trees now grown as large as the trees the cradles once carried. At the Chamberlain Lake end, the boilers and engine that powered the Tramway still stand, monuments to the Yankee ingenuity that created it and also, in a somewhat different way, to the invention that replaced it—the Lombard log hauler.

The Lombards were the first all-terrain vehicles in the North Woods. They were not tied to tracks, cables, and stationary engines. They were mobile and efficient, pulling a train of loaded pulp carriers behind them on iced trails through the woods. On an Allagash canoe trip in 1962, I saw my first Lombard. It was in an old barn at Churchill Depot at the headwaters of the Allagash River, about thirteen miles north of the Tramway. We opened the door, and there in the gloom permeated with a damp, aged-wood smell, I saw what I can best describe as an immense ghost-machine in the attic of the logging industry. Last year I saw another one abandoned near the bank of the lower Allagash River at the Cunliffe Depot Campsite. This was a smaller, later version, more technologically advanced.

On a timeline of uses of the Allagash from the disappearance of the last glacier some eleven thousand years ago to the present, these events in the history of the Allagash would be rather recent. I first saw other evidence of the waterway's history on that same 1962 canoe trip—flakes of Kineo rhyolite and Munsungun chert that had been worked by the hands of ancient toolmakers. The flint-like materials lay on a low, sandy shore along what was once the original Allagash River flowing between Chamberlain and Eagle Lakes. Later, in 1846, it became the site of a dam, called Lock Dam, that separated the two lakes. In 1962 the lakes below Chamberlain Lake were low because Churchill Dam had washed out several years before, leaving them at their pre-1846 level. I learned that our canoe party followed an ancient canoe route used for thousands of years by indigenous peoples. We found evidence of their presence all along our route through Eagle and Churchill Lakes. Years later when I accompanied the archaeologist David Putnam around Chamberlain Lake, we found more evidence of native encampment and toolmaking in front of Chamberlain Farm and at the Chamberlain Lake end of Mud Pond Carry, which funneled native canoeists from the Allagash lakes into the region of the West Branch of the Penobscot and vice versa. For me, these were exciting finds, especially since I could sit on the shores of the very lakes and streams these early people traveled and easily imagine their camps and the clicking of stone on stone as they patiently created their tools and other implements.

Today, these historic settings are protected: Maine in 1966 purchased a strip of land around these Allagash waters that by law is to be developed for its "maximum wilderness character," resulting, hopefully, in a return to a semblance of its once primitive condition. Already, nearly forty years later, the camps, log landings, roads, and other evidence of logging along the banks of the Allagash waters have nearly disappeared. Large trees now come once again to the water's edge, and in a few spots there are very old trees that somehow escaped the logging. As the decades pass, there will be many places along this canoe route where one can experience a strong feeling for the wild, natural setting first seen by the native people and later by the surveyors and loggers.

The lakes of the Allagash Wilderness Waterway lie in the shadow of the Katahdin range, and those who worked so hard for their preservation moved in the shadow of another preservationist—Governor Percival P. Baxter. Baxter singlehandedly saved Katahdin and the lands around it—more than 200,000 acres—completing his major acquisition four years before the Allagash was preserved. Few would question that Governor Percival Baxter was ahead of his time. That he was public-minded. That he cared about the woods, waters, and wildlife in his beloved state of Maine. That he cared about our relationship with the land. His gift to the people of Maine, most of which he left to be "forever wild," is today New England's largest wilderness area. This benevolent action set an example for our society to follow. He demonstrated that it is possible to save lands in the face of great odds. There is no question of his influence on those who sought to save the Allagash. All of the principal players had lauded his act, and most were acquainted with him. Today, while we still wait for someone in this generation who possesses Baxter's combination of values and financial resources to step forward and single-handedly match his gift, we are fortunate to have individuals and groups in this state of Maine who are inspired by Baxter's action and who in turn have inspired us with their own successes in the protection of land for the future.

Baxter State Park and the Allagash Wilderness Waterway are much more than first meet the eye. One must look at them closely to fully appreciate what they mean to us and future citizens. Both show us the reasons why it is in the best interest of our society to emulate these examples of preservation. For one, these wilderness areas allow us to understand more clearly the character of the landscape our ancestors faced, whether they were indigenous to this land or whether they came later from other places to settle and work. The Allagash and Baxter State Park are, in essence, living museums. And despite the fact that both were once cutover lands, a half-century of nature's healing already gives us the opportunity to take a trip back in time and begin to experience—to think and feel—what our ancestors did.

We have a highly regarded state museum here in our capital city of Augusta, a marvel really, for all who want to experience an accurate reconstruction of a way of life in our past. I still stand in awe at the sight of the restored Lombard log hauler at the museum's entrance, and I'm immensely fascinated by the expertly designed dioramas and displays of specimens in museum cases. These contribute greatly to our interest in and understanding of Maine's history, but Baxter and the Allagash preservationists taught us that we can also recreate natural settings that show what Maine's landscape once was, places that have become a living context for the artifacts of our history where we can explore the roots of our heritage in settings reminiscent of times past. Seeing artifacts of human interaction with the land in the places where they were used, especially places that have been allowed to return to an "original" wildness, cannot be duplicated.

Such settings, however, offer more. Embedded in these restored landscapes are signs of human attitudes and values toward nature. We are confronted, for example, with the mistakes we've made with the land. I remember hiking a trail that borders an eroded bank on a tributary of the Androscoggin River and seeing a layer of ash revealed in the soil beneath the roots of a blown-down tree, blackened rocks washed out of the crumbling slope on the river's edge, and bits of charcoal beneath a moss-covered log. All were signs of an extensive forest fire that swept through the area a century ago. Historic records suggest it was caused by human carelessness, and there is reason to suspect that it was fueled by slash from heavy clear-cutting on steeply sloped land. I have seen the deep gullies left from the runoff following this denuding of mountain sides and the ultimate uprooting of natural communities and displacement of their soils. I have seen the refuse of our civilization scattered in the woods we have worked. But I have also seen examples of other quite different attitudes and values in wilderness areas: evidence of reforestation, early facilities for wildlife management and protection, the removal of large dumps and deposits of refuse, the scarification and revegetation of no longer needed roads, and the sensitive design of unobtrusive trails.

When we see such signs in a landscape that we have allowed nature to reclaim, we are all the more inclined to reflect on our relationship with the rest of nature. We are prompted to ask ourselves why such a landscape was used and sometimes abused and to remember that these things occurred at a time when we thought that our resources were inexhaustible, that we could move on after we had plundered and befouled the land and waters in one place. We are encouraged to remember that our abuses didn't seem as threatening when our numbers on earth were small and we had much less technological ability to affect the health and sustainability of the land. We are also prompted to reflect on evidence that shows someone cared about the land—

to remember that there were those who were concerned about the loss of resources and the need to treat them in ways that would provide for the future. And, inevitably, we are forced to ask ourselves what is different today and how we should act toward our environment.

There are additional lessons that we can learn in reclaimed wild places. Often we can still see, even despite heavy use, remnants of an original nature. Clinging to steep slopes and other inaccessible terrain, a few patches of virgin forest might have managed to escape the logger's ax and saw, such as a stand of virgin spruce I once hiked through in Baxter State Park. Or on high mountain tops and steep-sided ledges and in deep ravines, communities of rare plants may have survived, such as the rare silverling, a low, tufted, silvery plant that I saw in the Caribou-Speckled Mountain Wilderness, once cutover and fire-swept land. In other places, one might discover small wetlands or waterfalls or a hidden layer of fossils or peculiar outcrops that evaded human disturbance, such as a historic ledge of ancient brachiopod fossils I photographed in the Allagash. Such places not only keep us in touch with those who first laid eyes on this land, but they also point to the marvelous diversity that we can allow to survive when we protect such areas. And they remind us by their rarity of how much we have lost.

Restored wild areas have other benefits. They are often in proximity to populated areas and are more quickly accessible for those who need a short-term respite from the pressures of civilization. They provide more convenient opportunities to be quiet, calm, and alone on remote trails and on patches of land evocative of an earlier, different time; to appreciate the awesome complexity, resiliency, and recuperative power of the natural world; and to be both humbled and uplifted. It is in such places that we can experience a renewal of the human spirit. Here we can become invigorated and empowered to think in fresh ways about our plans for the future, to contemplate our personal gifts and opportunities, and to see more clearly the steps we can take for a better life for ourselves, others, and our environment.

Today, we have an unprecedented opportunity to create new wilderness areas and capture their many potential values for present and future citizens. It is a time of changing economic conditions that are stimulating the selling and leasing of large tracts of our northern woodlands. But we also must be aware that today these lands are subjected to changes much more irreversible than at the time the Allagash Wilderness Waterway and Baxter State Park were set aside. Baxter, now the largest block of unroaded forest in Maine, was once crisscrossed by logging roads. But those roads were less permanent than today's logging roads, which are designed and built to meet the needs of modern forest-management regimens requiring frequent entry to forest stands. Thus, the amount of land where natural ecosystems and wilderness values are free and will remain free of the detrimental impacts of roads is shrinking. By one optimistic estimate, based on incomplete and dated data, only 2 percent of Maine land is in well-forested blocks greater than 1,225 acres in size and a little more than one-half mile from a road.★

Acquisition of some of our state's lands for wilderness areas, however, will not be inexpensive, nor will their management be as easy as the management of a museum housed in a building. We will need more than curators to manage areas we set aside as wilderness. We will need land stewards to actively manage their ecological health and promote respect for their boundaries. As in our museums, we must be concerned about carrying capacities and the behavior of visitors. These are manageable problems, and the many wilderness areas we already have provide many examples of what to do and not to do. And we have had people like Governor Percival Baxter who have shown us what is possible if we have the dream and the will to act.

★Jeffrey A. Hepinstall, et al., *Development and Testing of a Vegetation and Land Cover Map of Maine*, Technical Bulletin 173 (Orono, Maine: Maine Agricultural and Forest Experiment Station, University of Maine, 1999), 74–78.

DEAN BENNETT'S bio can be found on page 128.

Song For The Allagash

©2001
Alexandra S. B. Conover
For Wilmer Hafford

In the grand state of Maine, there's a
ri - ver_some know well, nine - ty miles it flows north, nine
hun - dred stories to tell, nine thousand years can-oes have
passed her wild shores, a pa - radise of si - lence for
travelers gone be - fore.

Punchy Refrain

Here's_to_the woods and the

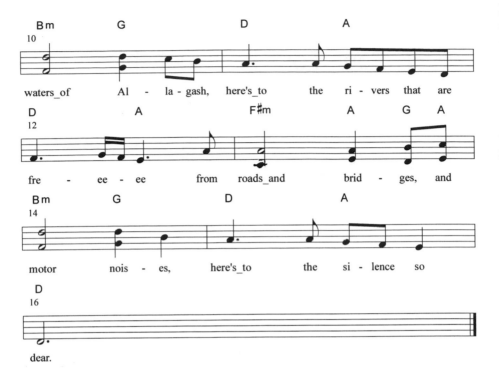

waters_of Al - la - gash, here's_to the ri - vers that are
fre - ee - ee from roads_and brid - ges, and
motor nois - es, here's_to the si - lence so
dear.

Well the Allagash country has fed our families
Native hunters and fishermen, their children running free
All the loggers and the guides, the river was their road
They all loved these waters that linked their work with home.

One day roads crept close to Allagash's shore
People came a-flocking with their motors, 'twas no chore
So easy and so free, driving in today
But a wild place is no longer if you can get there in one day.

We've got rivers a-plenty and lakes and ponds galore
There are roads to them all but some want even more
But there's only one place that the people agreed by law
To make a wild waterway for once and for all.

(With thanks to Margy Bray Leatham for preparing the musical
manuscript.)
ALEXANDRA CONOVER's bio can be found on page 14.

Borealis

Franklin Burroughs

I grew up in the South. The Deep North was one of the legendary geographies of childhood, like the Wild West or Darkest Africa. It reached me through tall tales, picture book stories about Paul Bunyan and Babe the Blue Ox, a weekly radio program about Sergeant Preston ("On King! On you huskies!") of the Yukon; through stories of Russell Annabel in *Sports Afield;* and through novelists like James Oliver Curwood (*Nomads of the North)* and Jack London (*White Fang*). Legendary geography nurtures a sense of possibility, escape, or homecoming. Children crave it; tourism sells it; most religions offer some version of it.

The Maine Woods were not my first or deepest encounter with the Deep North. That came in 1963, when I worked at a place called Cooper Lake, about 100 miles north of La Tuque, in the Province of Quebec. I worked for International Paper Company as a timber cruiser's assistant—a compass man. In 1963 La Tuque was the end of the road, at least of the paved and public road. Just beyond the town was a gate, the entryway to IP's huge leasehold, and access was strictly limited. Cooper Lake was about a half-day's trip over the rough logging road that ran northward from La Tuque.

A couple of dozen cruisers and compass men were based at Cooper Lake. I worked all summer with the same three of them, forestry majors at the University of New Brunswick. We spoke English. The others spoke French. None of us spent much time at Cooper Lake. We were flown out by float plane to what it would be silly to call a remote lake, because all the lakes except for Cooper Lake itself were remote, and some of the smaller ones were unnamed. The plane would take two of us out at a time, each time with a canoe lashed between the pontoons and half our gear stowed in back. On the first day, we'd pitch camp. That involved felling seven tall and slender spruce, limbing them, and making a frame of them, from which we suspended a big canvas wall tent. It involved digging a pit, filling it with stones, and then setting up a little collapsible box stove on top of the stones. It involved bucking up the wood we'd need for cooking, stashing the food where bears and lesser varmints couldn't get into it, and generally making things tidy and convenient.

On the subsequent days, we would go out—two in one direction, two in another—to a point on a map that had been randomly selected by somebody back at the home office in Montreal. There we would mark out a quarter-acre plot, count and measure each tree on it, and core and calculate the height of every ninth tree. Sometimes the spots were close by camp, but commonly it would take at least an hour of paddling and walking to reach them, and sometimes much more than that. We'd stay in that one camp for four or five days, until we had taken care of all the plots in its vicinity. Then the plane would come and take us back to Cooper Lake, where we would get to eat the hearty fare—stews, beans, pies, homebaked bread—that was standard at all the IP camps, take a shower, and sleep in a bunk for a night or two. Then we would go back out.

For the whole of that summer, I never knew what day of the week or the month it was, or cared. Time was a matter of daylight and of distance. Being a timber cruiser requires some skill and knowledge, but being a compass man does not. An English major could handle it; patiently and properly trained, a Labrador retriever could.

When the plane left us, we were on our own. The only human noise we heard was what we generated ourselves—the thunk of the ax, the click of the paddle against the gunwale. My cruiser had a harmonica, and liked to play it in the evening, after supper. The sound of it was miraculous in that unending emptiness, with the long twilight slowly fading out of the sky, and the chill coming out from the shadows. You understood the hunger for music, even of the most rudimentary sort.

It was genuine wilderness. We only once came across a habitation, although it would not be inhabited until winter. It was a trapper's cabin, stoutly built of unpeeled spruce logs and surrounded by a grove of dead spruce. The trapper had girdled them, so they'd die on their feet. It was explained to me that that was the smart way to do it. When the winter came, he wouldn't have to probe around in the snow to find his woodpile and then dig five or six feet down to reach it.

In June and July, it was hard to believe that the country could ever get that cold or be that bleak. The days went on forever. Water, seeping through vividly green and luxurious moss, was everywhere. To drink, you only had to part the moss, force a cup down into it, and watch the gin-clear, ice-cold water filter in. And the country swarmed with life—birds, insects, fish. In June I stepped into a brook and had the vertiginous experience of seeing its bottom dissolve like a cloud: spawning suckers—it was paved with them, packed thicker than Damariscotta alewives or Japanese commuters. But by late August we would paddle off to our day's work across gray lakes that were flecked with whitecaps, and sometimes we'd meet or be overtaken by quick gusting flurries of snow. The woods were quiet, the few remaining birds having grown furtive, all of them except the Canada jays, which got bolder and bolder as the summer receded.

The prevailing view was that all this would go on forever, that this forest was too big to worry about. If IP cut systematically northward from La Tuque, it would take decades to reach the timberline. By that time, the southern portion would have grown back to its original size, and they could start all over again. That is what I was told. I knew, even then, that the same arguments about North American inexhaustibility had proven themselves indisputably untrue in the Lower 48. But when we were being ferried by float plane from one lake to another, flying across ridges, lakes, rivers, muskegs, and, like a sea that surrounded and connected everything, the great sweep of coniferous forest, the lessons of the past were hard to take seriously. The skimpy little logging roads, the barracks-like camps where the loggers stayed, the scattered, slash-choked clearings, no bigger than so many postage stamps on the floor of a gymnasium, looked puny and ephemeral.

The Maine Woods were once part of this same boreal forest. Thoreau found north of Bangor something very much like what I found north of La Tuque. He was struck by the same above-ground aquifer of deep, spongy moss that covered so much of the forest floor, and by the pervasive dampness. He registered a complex sense of claustrophobia and loneliness, of delight in the sudden bright and breezy openings of lakes. He could not entirely resist a certain massive, implacable, and almost geological reduction of the solitary human consciousness, which he prized so deeply, to not much more than a flickering candle on a windy night. When I was in Quebec, I could not have admitted his ambivalence to myself, but when I read him, I knew that something like it had been there for me, part of the experience.

But to read Thoreau is also to recognize that even by 1850, the Maine Woods had been penetrated and altered by human purpose. He found pine stumps a span of oxen could stand and turn around on, but found no such stump with an actual pine tree still standing on it. He found streams that had been dammed and shunted, made into conveyor belts to take logs out to the Penobscot and down to Bangor. The woods I saw in Quebec were pretty much what they had always been; the only hydraulic engineering there was done by beavers.

So the history of logging here is very old by American standards—at least as old as the history of Maine as a political entity. You can get some idea of it by going to the logging museum northwest of Patten. And you can see how the technology of logging mirrors the technology of warfare. First it was a matter of muscle and leverage: teams of oxen and horses, pulling logs instead of caissons; crews of men traveling on foot, by rowboat or canoe, eating bad food, minimally sheltered against weather, disease, and exhaustion; horses, oxen, and men used hard, then replaced when they were used up. The first logging machines, steam-powered winches and skidders with steel treads, resemble the primitive and cumbersome tanks of the First World War. The chainsaw was to the northern forest what the machine gun was to the Western Front—a portable device that enormously multiplied the individual's destructive capability. Logging and warfare grew steadily more industrial and efficient during the twentieth century; the life of the individual logger or soldier, while still hard and dangerous, grew more and more to resemble the life of the ordinary industrial worker.

The history, or at least the archaeology, of logging is everywhere in the Maine Woods. Fishing on low water, you may still come across the rust-pocked point of a river driver's peavey, something that looks old and gruesome enough to have been wielded by an Orc or Viking. Remnants of roads run along most rivers. The woods have so overgrown them that at first they look merely natural and geological, like an esker. But here and there you come across a collapsed culvert or pick up the faint impressions of what were once deep ruts. Sometimes a single strand of wire, strung up about head high, runs along the road—a telegraph line, the communications technology of the Civil War adapted to the log drives. Here and there along a river you find the last rotting remnants of a sluice—a wooden aqueduct to carry logs over the jumbled terrain of a steep bank and down to the river itself. There are the collapsed remains of barns that sheltered horses, oxen, and hay, and are now havens for chipmunks and porcupines.

You are always stumbling across something—iron gear wheels and levers, indecipherable bits of extinct machines. At Nine Mile Bridge on the St. John, down off the old road and almost invisible in the undergrowth stands a steam-powered crane. It belongs in the museum in Patten but it also belongs where it is, peacefully rusting away. In this place, it looks historic and prehistoric, a hybrid begotten by James Watt upon a tyrannosaur.

The present reality of the Maine Woods is hideous swaths of clear-cut. It is log trucks, going from before dawn until after dark, the empty ones suddenly looming up in your rearview mirror like a blitzing linebacker, the laden ones laboring up the grade ahead of you, connecting *lumber* as a noun to *lumber* as a verb.

And the present reality is also assembly line tourism—downhill skiers, whitewater rafters, snowmobilers. The commercial infrastructure that houses, feeds, and amuses them has a substantial effect on the culture and environment of the North Woods, while minimizing the effect that the culture and environment have on them.

The future reality may be residential development, more and more lakes with more and more cottages on them. The greatly expanded network of logging roads has made more and more lakes and ponds accessible, and more and more people aware of them. If that development happens, it will be the end of the fact and the idea of the Maine woods. And that will have consequences for all of us who live here, whether we go Up North or not.

I moved to Maine five years after my summer in Quebec, to take a job at Bowdoin. I was serious, and seriously anxious, about the job. My wife and I were newly married, still learning how to live together. Living together in Maine, quite apart from Bowdoin and its community, suited us, and we realized that we did not want to live elsewhere or otherwise. The state seemed to marry a proximity to wildness, with all its sense of exploration and adventure, to some other sense of deep steadfastness, of settlements that had been made and balances that had been struck a long time ago. This was a model for any kind of marriage, a preserving of the adventure of trepidation and discovery in which it begins even as it grows rooted in the civilities, accommodations, and symbioses that are the causes and effects of its continuance.

A legendary geography starts by being something from long ago or far away that you hear about in childhood. It survives as a craving. If you are fortunate, you find an actual geography that nourishes and refines the craving. Sometimes in Maine you'll see a pickup truck with *I'd Rather Be Up North* stenciled neatly across the front, just over the grille. Saying that is different from saying that you'd rather be fishing or snowmobiling or skiing. *North* means north of where you are, in a place where life is cleaner and harder, possibly more retro and more macho, certainly freer, simpler, and sparser than it is where you live. In Maine, it conjures certain names, some for one person, some for another: the Golden Road, the Telos Gate, Hulling Machine Pitch, the Knife Edge, Spencer Rips, the West Branch, Wilson Hill Pond. These are definite places, and turn out to be exactly as prosaic as you yourself are, when you reach them. But people don't sound exactly matter of fact when they mention them. It is as though they were referring to celebrities they knew, not exactly boasting about their familiarity with them, but not exactly unimpressed by it either.

Maine's strangely historical backcountry has been and remains a commodity, something that can be bought, sold, or liquidated entirely. For a great many people in this corner of the country, it also has been and remains part and parcel of the shifting internal equilibrium that we call sanity. Sometimes it all seems robust, resilient, and indestructible; sometimes fragile, threadbare, hanging on by the skin of its teeth. All that we can take for granted is our responsibility to it—to the compromised, imperfect, beleaguered, and sustaining geographical fact of it, and to the vision of it as a place we'd rather be.

FRANKLIN BURROUGHS taught English literature at Bowdoin College from 1968 to 2002. He is the author of two books, *Billy Wattson's Croker Sack* and *The River Home*. His essays have appeared in a variety of literary quarterlies and have been reprinted in such collections as *Best American Essays, The Pushcart Anthology,* and *The Norton Anthology of Nature Writing.*

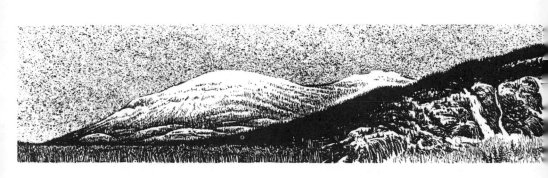

Upper South Branch Pond
Baxter Park

Jon Luoma

IN BEAVER COUNTRY, 1999

Christopher Huntington
Oil pastel on black paper, 22 x 30 inches

For me it has been impossible to escape the lure of the North, the sense of wild places that still belong to the Beaver, the Moose, and the Eagle. I have for forty years made a concerted effort to seek out pockets among the woods and boulders and dramatic sites along rivers that I can converse with in paint. *In Beaver Country* was done on location on black paper at the edge of a lumber road between Katahdin and Whetstone Falls on the East Branch of the Penobscot. I'm sure that my sense of the wilderness being in dire jeopardy informs the work I produce.

CHRIS HUNTINGTON's parents met at art school in Ohio, moving to Pemaquid in 1939 when he was eight months old. He didn't take up art until age twenty at Miami of Ohio University. Huntington is largely self-taught by painting from nature. He returned to Maine in 1962, where he painted a series of dark woodland streams. A move to North Belgrade was followed by three years as first curator at Colby College. From 1964 to 1976, he executed many oils at Shin Pond and Mt. Vernon, where he was in the antique business before he moved to Nova Scotia in 1974. In the early '90s, he returned to northern Maine, purchasing in 1997 a studio overlooking the Katahdin range near Patten.

Back Cover

THE OCTOBER TRIPTYCH, 1998

Marguerite Robichaux
Oil on birch, 60 x 96 inches

MARGUERITE ROBICHAUX's bio and statement can be found on page 96.